Chocoholic
Guilty of Loving a Black Man
By
D T Pollard
Essence Bestselling Author
Follow D T Pollard https://twitter.com/dtpollard

http://DTPollard.com

This is a work of fiction. All of the characters,
names, incidents, organizations and dialogue in this
novel are either the products of the author's
imagination or are used fictitiously.

Original non-text Image used on cover by

1

Ashley Riley wasn't thinking about developing a new marketing campaign for the next fashion line her company would introduce for the winter season as she was looking up at the ceiling illuminated by the soft flickering glow from candles sitting on nightstands positioned on each side of the king sized bed she was lying on. Although it was still over ninety degrees outside in the middle of summer in Dallas, Texas, cool air from the air conditioning vents flowed across her bare skin that was slightly tanned from lounging around the swimming pool of her friend Jerome's home. Ashley met Jerome one night at an after work gathering at a club in an exclusive hotel in north Dallas three months prior. After exchanging phone numbers, they had gone out several times and kept in contact quite often by talking on the phone and texting each other frequently. Ashley found Jerome to be intelligent, witty and confident. Ashley was twenty-eight years old, successful and beautiful. With her five-foot eight inch tall, toned and lean frame, quite a few eligible men at her company expressed a romantic interest in Ashley, but she was very reluctant to mix business with pleasure with a risky workplace relationship. Jerome finally invited Ashley over to his three thousand square foot home to spend the day on a Saturday and she accepted.

This was the first time she had been alone with Jerome outside of a public setting with others around. It had been a good day with good food, great wine and good conversation. Earlier when they sat next to each other on the sofa in the living room after the sun had gone down, Ashley decided it might be time to call it a day.

"Jerome, thanks for inviting me over today. I love your place and had a great time," Ashley said while taking a sip from a glass of wine.

"I'm glad you accepted my invitation and came over. I wanted to get some one-on-one alone time with you Ashley," Jerome said.

"Yeah, that was good. It's hard to really get to know someone with other people around all the time. It's starting to get late and before I drink too much, I think I need to get home," Ashley said as she stood to leave.

Jerome stood in front of Ashley and caressed her shoulders with both hands while looking into her deep blue eyes. There was a palpable tension in the air between them. Although they had gone out on several dates it was obvious that they were hesitant about crossing certain lines, but that time was about to end.

"Don't go," Jerome said as her pulled Ashley close to him and kissed her deeply.

Ashley realized that was the first time they had touched each other in an intimate manner.

Without hesitation Ashley returned Jerome's attention and then she felt his strong hands on her firm buttocks that were toned from a regular workout routine. Jerome's hands soon found new territory to explore as his right hand found its way under the front of her yellow sundress. Ashley ran her right hand across the front of Jerome's crotch covered by the thin material of his swimming shorts. Ashley's eyes widened when she felt the size and girth of his growing manhood. Before she realized what was happening, Jerome's wandering hand slipped inside the front of Ashley's small bikini bottoms she wore under her dress. Without protest Ashley aided Jerome's probing fingers by slightly parting her thighs. A gasp escaped her lips when Jerome's fingers made contact with her most sensitive private area. Ashley's wetness signaled her state of sexual excitement and she thrust her hips forward in response to Jerome's manual manipulations. Ashley wasn't one to be shy when she wanted something and she wanted this man.

"Damn Jerome what are you doing. Ohh shit, that feels good," Ashley admitted as she leaned her head backward.

"Have you ever been with a Black man before?" Jerome asked as he kissed Ashley on her neck.

"I prefer my men dark, the same way I like my coffee," Ashley informed after she had thrust her hand inside Jerome's shorts.

Jerome looked at Ashley, but he didn't say a word. Jerome then scooped Ashley up in his strong arms and carried her to his bedroom. Jerome placed Ashley on the bed and slowly removed their clothing. Jerome then lit candles that provided a soft romantic glow to the room and turned on soft music stored on his smart phone.

Ashley was impressed with Jerome who was a successful twenty-eight year old sales executive. Jerome had a muscular six foot tall frame, bright smile and kind brown eyes. Jerome crawled onto the bed from the bottom and Ashley gently parted her thighs. Ashley felt Jerome's hot breath and then the flick of his moist tongue on her sensitive sexual nerve center. A gasp escaped her lips as Ashley looked on when Jerome's dark brown right hand caressed her seemingly milky white breasts that were not tanned due to her bikini top blocking the sun earlier during the day. Ashley reached her hands down and caressed Jerome's smoothly shaved head nestled between her thighs.

"Oh yes Jerome. Lick it baby," Ashley uttered as she raised her knees and threw her head back.

Ashley began to move her pelvis up and down to meet Jerome's oral lovemaking rhythm.

Ashley was experiencing waves of pleasure shooting through her body when Jerome crawled up her torso and grasped the headboard of the bed with both hands. Ashley took Jerome's excited manhood in her hands and guided it into her eager mouth for her first taste of chocolate from this man. This was Jerome's first sexual encounter with Ashley, but he could tell she knew her way around a man's body.

"Oh shit!" Jerome exclaimed in response to Ashley's skillful manipulations.

Ashley brought Jerome to the edge of bliss before he quickly relocated his body so that he was kneeling between her legs. Jerome positioned Ashley's ankles at his shoulders and then he pressed her legs backwards as his throbbing member slowly eased her womanhood apart until the back of her thighs were touching the front of his.

"Oh my God baby!" Ashley said as she gently pressed the palms of her hands against Jerome's thighs so she could adjust her body.

Jerome paused and then began to rock Ashley's body as he repeatedly slammed into her while pressing her back into the 600 thread count Egyptian cotton sheets. With her arms spread out to her sides, Ashley clutched at the bed covers with her manicured fingernails.

"Fuck me Jerome! Fuck my White pussy baby!" Ashley encouraged.

Ashley was climbing her way to an explosive climax when she motioned for Jerome to turn over onto his back. Jerome complied and Ashley straddled his body with her back facing his face. Ashley slammed down onto Jerome's pelvic area while her hands gripped his ankles.

"Ride that black dick baby!" Jerome said.

Jerome's words seemed to send Ashley into overdrive and then she felt a slap on her right buttock from his hand that sent her over the edge. With perspiration dripping from her forehead, Ashley started to shake and pressed her pelvis down onto Jerome's body.

"Oh yes! Jerome! I'm coming baby!" Ashley said in almost a grunting voice.

"What the fuck is going on in here Jerome!" a female voice yelled as Ashley snapped her head around toward the bedroom door.

An attractive Black woman in her middle thirties was standing there with the handle of a roller equipped travel bag in one hand. Ashley was confused and almost in shock, but she instinctively rolled off the bed onto the floor on the side that placed it between the woman and her.

"Vaneshia, what, what are you doing here?!" Jerome said with a stutter.

"Jerome, who is this?! What's going on?!" Ashley asked excitedly.

"Who am I?! I'm his fiancée! Who the fuck are you, White bitch?!" Vaneshia asked almost screaming

"Fiancee! Jerome, you said you weren't seeing anybody!" Ashley said in surprise.

"Uh huh. Your lying ass got caught again, didn't you Jerome! You thought I would still be with my mother in Arkansas, but she got better faster than we thought and I came back early to surprise you. I even stopped by that little erotic store on the way back and bought a few things for us. I got some flavored oils, some edible panties and some lube, but I see you already got you some White pussy before I got back! I loved you Jerome and did everything for you! I took your ass back, bought you a car and I paid all the bills! What else do you want?! Am I too old for you?! What is it?! First it was that big tittied little young dumb ass high school educated bitch from the supermarket and now this White hoe! Not only that, but you fucked this bitch in my house and in my bed! Jerome, you're lucky I'm saved or both of you might be dead motherfuckers by now! I've got my piece right here in my purse," Vaneshia said with tears flowing.

Vanishia reached into her purse and pulled out a pistol. Vaneshia didn't point the gun at Jerome, but she held it up and looked it over.

"You know Jerome I could shoot both of your asses and get away with it. Have you ever heard of a crime of passion? You know when somebody is so shocked by something that they temporarily lose their mind. I think walking in my bedroom and finding my fiancée fucking another woman in my bed might qualify," Vanisha said as she pointed the gun toward Jerome's head.

"Vaneshia please! I'm sorry baby!" Jerome said pleadingly.

"Please don't," Ashley pleaded.

"Fuck you nigga! Jerome, I'm not throwing my life away by putting a cap in your bitch ass! Don't worry Becky, or whatever your name is, I'm not blaming you, because he lied to you just like he does to everybody else. I'm leaving for about two hours and Jerome, when I get back I want you and all your shit out of my house! I should have known better than to take your cheating ass back from the last time I caught you fucking that little thot cashier that worked at the grocery store! That little bitch was always smiling in your face, but at least you didn't bring her into my house. You may as well go ahead and finish fucking this little White hoe since you lied to her too, but know this bitch, all this shit here is mine, you can have his broke ass!" Vaneshia said through tears as she put her gun back in her handbag, turned and walked away.

During the entire heated exchange between Vaneshia and Jerome, Ashley was looking over the side of the bed with her eyes just above the edge.

Vaneshia then stopped in the hallway, took a plastic bag out of a side pocket on her bag and threw it onto the bed.

"Jerome that's the stuff I bought at the erotic store. You can use it on that little slut if you want to because you sure won't need it for me!" Vaneshia said and then she turned and left.

"You lied to me! I could have been killed!" Ashley said furiously.

"I'm sorry Ashley! I didn't mean to hurt you!" Jerome said.

Ashley looked over at Jerome as she was putting her clothes on quickly.

"Hurt me? It's not like we were getting married or anything, but I don't want to get shot over a good fuck! What if she had flipped out and pulled the trigger! So, this isn't even your house?!" Ashley asked.

"No, this is Vaneshia's place. I guess I'll go over to my mother's house and stay," Jerome said.

"What! Are you even in sales like you told me?" Ashley asked.

"Yeah, but I sell insurance in a call center, not software like I told you," Jerome admitted.

Ashley was fuming by that time.

"You lying motherfucker! Don't call me! Don't text me! Erase my number from your phone!" Ashley said as she was heading for the front door.

Jerome followed behind her without a stitch of clothing on.

"Come on Ashley. You were having a good time, you know, until Vaneshia came in. Maybe we could go over to your place," Jerome said.

Ashley stopped in her tracks almost not believing what she just heard

"What! Fuck you!" Ashley said as she walked out of the front door and slammed it behind her.

Ashley got into her new blue Jaguar and drove away from the house she thought belonged to a man that could have been the one, but now she was left feeling empty after sharing her most personal gift with him and wasting three months of her life on a pretender. As she drove tears rolled down Ashley's face. For the first time in a while Ashley felt she needed to take some time off from work and go home to visit her parents that lived on the Gulf Coast of Texas.

2

Ashley went to work on Monday morning and her friend Janeka, who was the sales director for the company, was eager to hear all about her date with Jerome. Janeka was a classic Black beauty with a build that was the opposite of Ashley, Janeka was about five feet five inches tall with dark brown skin, high cheek bone structure and plump lips. Janeka had a narrow waist that seemed even slimmer due to her 34 DD breasts and protruding ass that caused many men to comment that she had a perfect donk that they loved to watch walk away from them. Janeka also had legs with prominent calf muscles that were accentuated by the five inch heels she preferred to wear. Janeka walked into Ashley's office and sat down in front of her desk.

"Why didn't you call me and let me know how things went with Jerome on Saturday? You know I was dying to find out, unless you stayed over on Sunday too," Janeka said with anticipation.

Ashley ran her hands through her hair and looked down at her desk.

"Close the door," Ashley requested and Janeka oblidged.

"I know that look. What the hell happened?" Janika asked.

"Well things were going great. We spent the day together and had a great time. It was starting to get late and I stood up to leave and then her kissed me and, you know, things felt right and we ended up in bed," Ashley said.

"Oh my God, so you fucked," Janika said.

"Yeah, we fucked," Ashley confirmed.

"So what was the problem? Did he suck at it, have a little dick or was he a minute man?" Janika asked.

"No, it wasn't any of that. It was great. I had a great time and I was trying to break it off when his fiancée walked into the room," Ashley informed.

Janeka sat there in stunned silence.

"What! His fiancée, what fiancée?!" Janeka asked.

"That's what I asked. He told me he wasn't seeing anyone," Ashley said.

"Hold up! She walked into the room. So, what were you doing when she walked in?" Janeka quizzed.

"I was on top of him. I mean I was in the middle of coming when I heard her. I mean I didn't know what the hell was going on, so I rolled off his ass onto the floor," Ashley said.

"Holyshit! Did she jump your ass?!" Janeka asked.

"No, but she pulled a gun on him," Ashley said.

"Holy shit!" Janeka exclaimed.

"I was scared shitless, but she didn't shoot his sorry ass. Apparently he has a history of lying and cheating. She left and told him to be gone by the time she got back. He lied to me about everything. His job, his relationship status and of course it was her house and not his. I was so pissed off. I felt like a fool. I need a break to clear my head. I'm taking Thursday and Friday off and going to my parents' house down in Galveston," Ashley said.

"It's that bad?" Janeka asked.

"I need to get my shit together. I want to find someone I can count on. I don't want to still be dating ten years from now," Ashley said.

"Are you thinking about trying vanilla instead of chocolate?" Janeka asked.

"No that's not what I mean. You know I prefer Black guys. I just haven't found the right one," Ashley said.

"Yes, I know you do. I don't understand it, but I know. Look it's hard enough for me as a black woman to find a good black man that's not paying child support, has a criminal record or is married if he's desirable. Most of the brothers I know that have everything I want in a man have a string of women after them and they are taking advantage of it. I'm not going to be on a dick rotation schedule waiting my turn for some man to get around to me. I think I'm worth more than that," Janeka said.

"Is it that bad? So what are you going to do?" Ashley asked.

"I'm thinking about broadening my horizons and start dating men outside of my race," Janeka replied.

"Really? I don't know why I said that. I do it all the time," Ashley said.

"I don't know how you do it. It feels scary to me. I mean with a Black guy I feel like I'm in a certain comfort zone in what I can say, where I can go and not feel like I'm going to offend him or stick out like a sore thumb. Do you know what I mean?" Janeka asked.

"I understand what you're saying. I do feel a little funny if the guy I'm with uses the n-word and know I can't say it like he can, but I don't mind being different than most of the other people in the room," Ashley admitted.

"Look, I've got to get to work. I'll see you again before you leave," Janeka said as she left Ashley's office.

Thursday morning came very quickly and before she knew it Ashley was driving south on Interstate 45 which is the main thoroughfare between Dallas and Houston. Although not a particularly scenic drive, it was long enough to allow Ashley to clear her mind. As the miles melted away, Ashley found herself singing along with one of her favorite songs blasting from her car's sound system. Ashley's singular karaoke act was interrupted when a phone call came in over her vehicle's audio system that was connected by bluetooth to her mobile phone. The name that displayed on the digital display in the middle of her console surprised her; it was James Thomas, a man she was once in love with before she moved to Dallas.

"Hello," Ashley answered.

"Hello Ashley, it's James," he said.

"James, how are you? I'm so surprised to hear from you," Ashley said.

"I know. I was hoping you still had the same phone number. Listen, are you in town?" James asked.

"Well actually, I'm driving down to my parents in Galveston, are you in Dallas?" Ashley asked.

"I'll be in Dallas next week. I may be taking over as the branch manager for our Dallas office and will be there to review the operation. If you're back in town, I would love to see you to catch up on old times," James informed.

"Sure, I'll be back by then. Give me a call when you know your schedule and we can set something up," Ashley said.

"That sounds great. Be safe. Bye Ashley," James said.

"Bye James," Ashley replied.

Ashley hadn't spoken to James in the six years since he got married and just the thought of seeing him again made her heart race. James wanted Ashley to go with him to New York when they graduated college, but she wanted to take a job offer in Texas, so they cried and parted ways. James fell in love with another woman and Ashley actually attended his wedding. Ashley always wondered what might have been. Ashley tried to forget about James and concentrated on the road ahead because she had two hours to go and needed to be on her toes when she drove through Houston with its bustling traffic on her way to Galveston. After clearing the traffic of the big city, James popped into Ashley's thoughts again, but she was sure he just wanted to say hello since he was married and probably had children since they parted ways. Ashley's thoughts turned to seeing her parents when she saw the bridge that connected Galveston Island to the mainland of the United States with water on both sides.

A smile came across Ashley's face since she was almost at her parents' house, but this was not where she grew up as her mother and father relocated after she went to college. Ashley grew up in the deep east Texas city of Lufkin, in the heart of the piney woods and that experience shaped how she viewed the world. Ashley was the youngest of three children and was the first to attend college as her two older brothers enlisted in the military. Ashley worked hard in school, got good grades and earned a partial academic scholarship, when combined with federal grants, allowed her to enroll in college in Florida. Ashley attended a historically black college, Florida Agricultural and Mechanical University, which was also a state school. Ashley noticed James one night as she watched him practicing with the band as one of their drum majors. Ashley saw the street her parents lived on and made a right turn before pulling into their driveway three houses down on the right side of the street.

"There she is! My big city girl!" Ashley's father Edward said while he was trimming the grass by the flowerbed.

"Hi dad!" Ashley said as her father gave her a big hug and kiss.

"How you doing kid?" Edward asked.

"I'm fine, but it's too hot for you to be out here at your age," Ashley said.

"At my age! Ashley, I'm only fifty-seven! I took a couple of days off so we could spend some time together. Your mother is in the house cooking your favorite meal," Edward said.

"Spaghetti with hot Italian sausage and her special seasoning?! Oh, I love that, but it not good for my figure," Ashley said.

"Your figure, you could use some meat on your bones. I heard those Black guys you like prefer a little more junk-in-the-trunk than you've got," Edward said without cracking a smile.

"Dad, that's not nice. We can talk about that later, but I know you have issues with my choice in men, but I just want to relax while I'm here, please," Ashley informed.

"I'm sorry, that was mean. Let's go inside. It is kind of hot out here," Edward said.

Ashley went inside and greeted her mother Katherine and got a whiff of the meal she was preparing. After taking a shower to refresh from her trip Ashley sat down with her parents for a home cooked meal.

"Mom, you've still got it. This is delicious," Ashley said after downing a forkful of spaghetti.

"I'll never forget how to cook. I have your father's dinner ready for him every day when he gets home," Katherine said.

"Dad you know that younger women don't do that anymore, so don't get any ideas if some young thing winks at you. She just wants your retirement money and for you to take her out to eat all the time," Ashley said.

"You don't have to worry about that. They don't make women like your mother anymore. She's stuck with me through thick and thin and there was a lot of thin, even when you were growing up," Edward said.

"So Ashley, are you seeing anybody special, you know a man?" Katherine asked.

"No, not really, it's hard with my work schedule, but I do want to settle down and have kids, eventually," Ashley said.

"Maybe if you expanded your horizons a little, it would make it easier, you know, more choices," Edward said.

"Ed, please! Not now," Katherine said.

"No mom. It's okay. We may as well talk about this right now. So, dad, by expanding my horizons, you mean start dating White guys, right?" Ashley said.

"Yes, that's what I mean. Ashley, I just don't understand why you don't go out with White men," Edward stated.

"No dad, what you really what to know is why do I only go out with Black men. Why does that bother you so much?" Ashley asked.

"I just don't understand it. Can you help me understand it?" Edward implored.

"Oh dad, I just wish you would accept me like I am and the choices I make, but since this bothers you so much, I'll try to make you understand. You know when we were living in Lufkin and going through some of those thin times you were talking about, I was having a really hard time in school, you know. I never told you or mama about it, but the other White kids called me trailer trash, because we lived in that run down old mobile home in that field. We were poor and they considered me to be White trash and not good enough to be their friend. I didn't wear fancy clothes or makeup, because we couldn't afford it. They didn't want anything to do with me, especially the girls. The White guys, as I got older, started to pay me some attention, but they just wanted to use me. They thought that just because I was poor that I would let them do whatever they wanted, you know, like having sex with them in secret while they took the popular girls out on dates. They asked me to go with them to some out of the way place or off somewhere at night when a football or basketball game was going on at school so they could have sex with me. Some of them even asked if they could come by to see me on the weekends while you were working. I guess they thought I didn't have any self-respect because of what they thought of me and wanted their approval so bad that I would do anything to get it, including letting them use me like that. I knew of a few girls that fell for that, but I wouldn't do it," Ashley said.

"Ashley, I had no idea the other kids were treating you that way. Why didn't you tell us?" Edward asked.

"I didn't want you and mom to feel bad because I knew you were working hard, but not making a lot of money working those low paying jobs. I didn't want you to feel like it was your fault," Ashley said with tears rolling down her face.

"Oh honey," Katherine said as she hugged her daughter.

"Well anyway, I was being picked on one day when I was in the fifth grade by Rebecca Strickland in the cafeteria because I wanted to sit with them at lunch. She called me trashy Ashley," Ashley informed.

"Are you talking about John Strickland's daughter? He owned the poultry processing plant I was working at. That little bitch!" Edward said.

"Ed, please!" Katherine said.

"Sorry," Edward said.

"Well, this black girl, Latrisha Johnson, told Rebecca to leave me alone and told me I could eat with them. She wasn't afraid of Rebecca and became one of my best friends. Her father hauled pulpwood, so I guess you can say he worked for himself. From that time on, I hung around with the black kids. They didn't judge me or look down on me because of where I lived or how much money my parents made. They saw me. Dad they saw me as a person, not my social status or economic status, but me as a person. Latrisha is the reason I studied so hard in school. I was over at her house studying one day and her mother told her she had to be twice as good as someone White to get the same job because she was Black and a girl. They were in the kitchen and I was in the living room, but I heard her say that. I wasn't Black, but I was a poor White girl, so I figured I needed to be twice as good as any man to compete with him for a good job too," Ashley said.

"I always wondered why you studied so hard. I barley finished high school and your father dropped out in the eleventh grade to help his family out. We were working all the time to keep a roof over our heads and food on the table. We should have done better on pushing you to do good in school, but we just didn't know what to do or even how to help you with your homework," Katherine admitted.

"I know you guys did the best you could, it was just tough back then. I was never cold, hungry or unsafe. We loved each other and had fun, but things were rough. Now that I'm grown I can look back and see that the economy was in bad shape. Right before I graduated high school, the recession hit, so I knew I had to be able to take care of myself, get a good education and get a good job. Well anyway, since my friends were Black, when I started going out, I went out with Black guys. I never told you that because I didn't know how you would feel about it, but they treated me nice. I listened to Black music, knew all the dances they did and I was more comfortable around Black people socially than White people. I was comfortable with the African American culture and that's why I only date Black men," Ashley explained.

"Then you went to that Black college in Florida," Edward said.

"Well, that's where I got my scholarship and grants. It's a historically Black university, but it's a state school and there were a lot of White people there too when I went. Latrisha went there and I applied when she did. It was great for me because I didn't know a lot about anything and they had smaller classes and helped me get adjusted. I didn't know anything about the business world, how to talk in front of a group of people or stuff like that. A lot of the kids that went to school there came from backgrounds where their parents never went to college or didn't own businesses, so they had programs designed to get them ready for the corporate world. I was no different than those other kids," Ashley said.

"That's where you met that guy you moved in with, that we didn't know about," Edward said.

"You mean James. Yes, that's where I met James," Ashley said.

"Ashley, we came to your graduation and you introduced us to him. We had no idea you were living with somebody, let alone a Black man. I was a little shocked," Edward said.

"I'm sorry I never told you what was going on, but do you understand why I feel the way I do?" Ashley asked.

"I guess I understand, but I'm not going to lie and say I'm happy about it. It's just not something I can think about and be okay with. You're my daughter!" Edward said.

"Dad, why do you have such a problem with this? Didn't you vote of President Obama twice? He's a Black man," Ashley pointed out.

"That's different. He was running the country, had a family and wasn't sleeping with my only daughter," Edward said.

"Is that what you're worried about, Black men with their hands on me and having sex with me? Dad it doesn't rub off and show in public or make me damaged goods," Ashley said sobbing.

"Honey I know, but you know. You hear stories about how White women are treated by Black guys, you know, when they are with them. I'm just concerned," Edward said.

"What? Dad I'm not going to do anything I don't want to do. I don't do orgies or stuff like that if that's what you're worried about. I'm not a slut letting Black men run trains on me. You raised me better than that and I don't deal with thugs or hang out at drug houses. I deal with respectable people Dad!" Ashley said still distraught.

"I'm sorry, I know you do. It's just hard to get used to," Edward admitted.

"Dad, have you ever thought about slavery?" Ashley asked her father.

"Slavery, what does that have to do with anything?" Edward asked puzzled.

"Well, I took an African American history class in college. The Black women that were slaves were treated terribly. The White slave owners would force them to have sex with them whenever they wanted. It was basically rape on demand. It didn't matter if they were underage, married or had children, there was nothing they could do about it, because they were property, those White men owned them, but because of that horrible situation, we probably have African American relatives we don't know about. Even though they were having their way with their Black slave women, the slave master's biggest nightmare was their White wives and daughters being with a Black man. I hope you don't think that way. We are all the same inside. No one owns me dad. No one is forcing me to do anything against my will, but I do have a question for you," Ashley stated.

"What's that?" Edward asked.

"If I fell in love and married a man and he happened to be Black, would you accept him into the family as your son-in-law?" Ashley asked.

"Yes, If you love him and he made you happy, of course I would accept him," Edward said.

"Thank you. If I had children with that man, would you love them?" Ashley inquired.

"Of course I would love them. Your kids would be my blood. My grandchildren," Edward said.

"Thanks Dad. You know I love you. You're just old fashioned," Ashley said as she hugged him.

"Ashley, I'm trying to catch up with this new world we're living in. Your Uncle found a better job for me down on the docks and things have been better since we moved. We're not White trash or trailer trash and never were. That Rebecca Strickland was dumber than a box of rocks. She ran her father's company into the ground after he had a stroke and the USDA shut them down. You're doing better than most of those people that were looking down on you anyway. You're smart, beautiful and have a good job. We're very proud of you," Edward said.

"Thank you. I'm glad you understand where I'm coming from," Ashley said.

"Ashley you mentioned something about wanting children. I hope you find somebody soon and get married. I need me some grand babies. Your brothers are all over the world in the service and haven't slowed down long enough to get married or anything. I'm not getting any younger, I'm just saying," Katherine said.

"Okay mom. I hear you, but you are going to have to wait a little while longer. I have to find a man first, fall in love and then have children," Ashley said with a laugh.

Ashley felt relieved after completing the most adult conversation she ever had with her parents about her preference for Black men and in the process let them know about events in her past that shaped her view of the world and relationships. Ashley was able to enjoy the rest of her visit with her parents since the elephant in the room had been addressed. All too soon Ashley was pulling out of her parent's driveway and heading back to Dallas feeling renewed. For the three days she was with her parents, Ashley had no thoughts of work or deceitful men on her mind as she ran along the seawall every morning and listened to the waves break on the beach in solitude. As she drove northward, thoughts of seeing James again dominated her mind and filled her with anticipation.

3

"I had the strangest talk with my parents. We discussed why I only go out with Black men," Ashley said.

"What! How the hell did that come up?" Janeka asked as she sat across from Ashley's desk.

"My father had a real problem with me dating Black men. Well, I think he had a bigger problem with me dating Black men exclusively. I think it helped me just as much as it helped them, so I could remember how I got to be who I am," Ashley said.

"How did it go? Did they understand?" Janeka inquired.

"They understood. I don't think mama cares who I like, she just wants some grandchildren, but I can tell it still bothers my dad. I think he has these images in his head of some big Black man defiling his pure white daughter with his massive black tool. I understand it. It's racial, tribal and as old as the ages, but he'll have to accept it. I have to be myself and that's part of who I am," Ashley said.

"Damn girl. You're something else. So what do you do now since Jerome turned out to be a lying fraud?" Janeka asked.

"I don't know. I may just take a break and let someone find me. I did hear from my old college boyfriend James. He called me when I was on my way to my parents. It looks like he may be moving to Dallas and wants to meet for dinner or something," Ashley said.

"Is there still something there between you?" Janeka asked.

"He's married. I think he just wants to catch up on old times. I mean we did live together and it was serious, really serious. James wanted me to go to New York with him after college, but I took a job offer I had here. I didn't want to pass up a good job, because I knew I had to support myself. I didn't want to depend upon him without a sure job waiting for me in New York and going to live with my parents was not an option. I think it really did a number on him and I really wanted to go. I loved him, but I was scared. Anyway, he met somebody else and got married," Ashley said.

"Oh well, at least you'll get to see him again. I'll see you later," Janeka said as she got up and left.

Ashley checked her schedule and she had a meeting she needed to get to regarding planning for the winter product line launch. As Ashley entered the board room she noticed the new merchandising manager, Chase Hanson, talking with Jason Nelson the retail manager for the southern zone. Chase was new to the headquarters office and came in when Ashley was out of town the week prior. Chase was twenty-nine years old, single and quite handsome.

With a six foot one inch tall, slim athletic build, chiseled chin and radiant smile, Chase was the topic of discussion of many of the single women around the office. Chase took notice of Ashley when she walked by. Ashley was an attractive woman and with her form fitting above the knee length dress, five inch heels and crisp hairstyle with blonde highlights she caught Chase's eye.

"Who's that?" Chase asked Jason.

"That's Ashley Riley, our marketing director. She was out when you came in last week," Jason said.

"Oh yeah, someone mentioned her. Is she married or involved with someone? She's hot," Chad asked.

Little did Chase or Jason know that Ashley was sitting near the door just out of their sight, but their voices carried farther than they thought and her ears perked up when she heard her name mentioned. Ashley listened to see what they were discussing that concerned her.

"Yes she is, but cool your jets, you're not her type. I know. I tried," Jason informed.

"What does that mean? Ohh, she's lesbian. Damn, what a waste," Chase said.

"No, she's not lesbian, she likes men," Jason said.

"Okay, then I'll see if she was to grab lunch, coffee or something," Chase said.

"You, my friend, don't have enough melanin in your skin for her liking," Jason said.

"Melanin in my skin? You lost me," Chase said.

"More melanin makes your skin darker. Ashley likes Black guys," Jason informed.

"Ohh, she's one of those. Got you," Chase said.

Ashley heard every word and was furious that Jason would discuss her personal business with a work colleague who didn't know her. If she desired to, she could fry Jason for creating a hostile work environment with his discussion of her preference in men with a coworker, but that was not the way Ashley handled things. Ashley left her seat and walked up to Chase.

"Hi Jason and you must be Chase, the new southern zone merchandising manager. I'm Ashley Riley, the marketing manager. Do you want to grab a cup of coffee after the meeting to discuss what you have in mind for the southern zone so we can get an idea of how to tweak the marketing plan to meet the unique needs of that market?" Ashley asked.

"Oh, yeah, that would be great," Chase answered while looking at Jason.

"Fantastic, we can hit the coffee shop downstairs. It looks like the meeting is about to start. We'd better get in there," Ashley said as she walked into the boardroom.

Chase turned to Jason.

"Maybe it was you," Chase said.

Ashley had no interest in Chase, but could not pass up the opportunity to stick it to Jason to pay him back for discussing her personal life out of turn. After the meeting and coffee discussion with Chase, Ashley was headed out to meet Janeka for lunch when her phone received an incoming call from James.

"Hello," Ashley answered.

"Hello Ashley. It's James, how are you?" James asked.

"I'm doing great, how about you?" Ashley inquired.

"I'm fine. Listen, I will be in town Friday morning and wondered if you would like to meet for dinner Friday night?" James asked.

"Sure, that will be great," Ashley replied.

"Okay. I don't have a restaurant picked out, but I will text the information to you. It will be good to see you again," James said.

"Okay. I'm looking forward to it. Bye," Ashley replied and ended the call.

Ashley continued on to lunch, but she had butterflies in her stomach over the prospect of seeing James again. In reality, Ashley didn't know how James really felt about her after she refused to go to New York with him after they graduated from college. James never knew it, but six months after they parted ways, Ashley was about to call him and try to rekindle their relationship when he called her just to keep in touch. During that prior conversation James casually mentioned to Ashley he had met a woman he was interested in, but it was early in their relationship and they were just getting to know each other. Ashley congratulated James and wished him good luck and apparently things went well because eight months later he married Shenita Johnson. Ashley attended James' wedding and met Shenita, who was a beautiful, intelligent and proud Black woman. Ashley felt that Shenita and James made a great couple and loved each other, but when she saw James kissing Shenita during the wedding ceremony her heart skipped a beat over what could have been. Two days later Ashley received a text message from James with information on where they would meet for dinner.

Ashley managed to get through the rest of her work week and at the end of the day on Friday, she went home to get ready to see James for the first time in years. As Ashley put the final touches on her hair and makeup a feeling of guilt came over her for being so concerned about how she looked before meeting a married man, but after checking the mirror, she thought she looked fantastic. With her dark red lipstick, long neck and trim figure, Ashley look more like a runway model than someone that hailed from a beat up mobile home sitting in a field. Ashley left her uptown Dallas condominium and started the drive to meet her old college flame for dinner.

4

Ashley pulled up to valet parking in front of the restaurant where she was meeting James for dinner. After Ashley walked inside, she spoke to the hostess and gave the name of who she was meeting. Ashley was led to a corner booth. When she came into view, James stood to his full six-foot two inch height, stepped out and kissed Ashley on the cheek. Seeing James was a jarring experience for Ashley. The years had been good to him as he now looked more polished, somewhat bulkier than before and was still as handsome as ever.

"Wow Ashley, you look great. It's so good to see you," James said as they sat down.

"You're looking pretty good yourself, Mr. Thomas. You've put on a couple of pounds," Ashley observed.

"It's all muscle," James said with a laugh.

"Oh really," Ashley said with a smile.

"How are you doing?" James asked.

"I'm doing great. I love my job, my condo and everything is going great," Ashley said.

"How about you?" Ashley asked.

"I'm doing great. I've decided to take the Dallas branch manager's position, so that's a big step up," James said.

"That's great, I'm sure you will do a awesome job. Is Shenita excited about moving to Dallas?" Ashley asked.

Just then the waiter came by and they placed their dinner and drink orders.

"Well, Shenita is not coming. We've been divorced for two years," James said.

"What?! Oh James, I'm so sorry. I had no idea," Ashley said.

"I am too, but you know that happens about half the time in this country. It's one of the reasons I decided to take this position. I can kind of get a fresh start here," James said.

"James, look, I don't want to pry, but what happened? You guys were crazy about each other," Ashley asked.

"I'll tell you, but not in a place like this. You never know who's listening," James said.

"I understand," Ashley said.

Although Ashley said she understood why James didn't want to discuss the reasons for his divorce, she was dying of curiosity inside to know what happened.

"What about you? You said your career is zooming, but I didn't hear about anybody special in your life," James said.

"There's a reason for that. There is no one special, but I've got a story to tell you that I don't want to talk about in public too," Ashley said.

"Now you've got me curious," James said.

The rest of the night was filled with small talk and all too soon they were about to say goodbye as they stood outside the restaurant by the valet parking area waiting for their vehicles to be brought around.

"James, are you doing anything in particular tomorrow?" Ashley asked.

"No, not really. I don't go into the office until Monday, so I was just going to hang out at the hotel or catch a movie to pass the time," James said.

"Why don't you come over to my place instead of sitting around that hotel? I can grill some steaks, Texas style of course and we can watch some movies, talk or see some sights if you want. I live close to downtown," Ashley said.

"That sounds a lot better that what I was planning. Text me the time and address and I'm there. What should I wear?" James asked.

"James, this is Texas in the middle of the August and it's a zillion degrees outside. Wear shorts or something light and comfortable. You're from Shreveport and know how hot it gets down here," Ashley said.

"Yeah, I know. I'll look for your text. See you tomorrow," James said as he got in his rental car that was brought around.

Ashley watched James drive away and then got into her car that was behind his. While driving home Ashley had all manner of thoughts going through her mind. Ashley felt confused and conflicted. Seeing James again was different that she thought it would be. Ashley realized the James she knew was years removed from the man she met for dinner and she was also a different person from the young woman he once knew. After she got home, Ashley sent a text message to James with her address and asked him to come over at two o'clock in the afternoon.

The next day Ashley spent the day preparing for James to come over and part of that preparation was a shopping trip to gather everything she needed to put together a good meal. Ashley would grill the food on one of the gas grills located by the swimming pool that was on the third floor of the condominium building. Ashley lived on the twentieth floor of the high-rise structure.

Ashley donned a pair of casual white shorts, open toe sandals and a blue short-sleeve top. James called and Ashley buzzed him into the building. Once James arrived at her door, Ashley made frozen margaritas for both of them before they headed to the pool and grilled the food. Once back inside they ate and sat facing the balcony that provided a view to the west toward Fort Worth. The white arch of the Margaret Hunt Hill Bridge was in full view and to the south they could see the familiar Reunion Tower structure that so many around the world associate with the city of Dallas.

"I really like your place Ashley. This is a great location, you know, to look out and reflect on things," James said.

"Thank you. I love it here. You know when we had dinner last night, you said you didn't want to discuss what happened with your marriage in public," Ashley reminded.

"Well it's complicated. You know I was so excited to go to New York, except for the fact that you didn't come with me, but after I got there, I was determine to make it. The last thing I wanted was to fall on my face and end up back home in Shreveport. Some of my family thought I was trying to be some kind of baller by moving to the big city. One of my sisters had the nerve to tell me I thought I was better than the rest of them because I got my degree and didn't come back home, but anyway I went all in at work. I did whatever it took to make my sales quota. I went in early and stayed late, you know whatever it took. You know when you're young, single and full of ambition, you can burn some of that extra energy since you don't have a family or kids at home waiting on you to come home from work. When I met Shenita she was drawn to my drive and desire to be successful. She knew how hard I worked and enjoyed the perks it provided so when we got married I thought she

41

understood what it took for me to provide the lifestyle we enjoyed. I mean, financially, it's no joke to live in the New York area. She began to complain about how much time I spent at work, but I told that that it was better for me to go all in now to get ahead before we had kids and then I could slow down, but would be in a better financial position. She said she understood," James said.

"So what changed?" Ashley asked.

"While I was working late and getting closer to my goals, like this promotion, Shenita was getting closer to someone else, her exercise class instructor," James said.

"James, are you telling me that Shenita cheated on you?" Ashley said in surprise.

"Well yeah, that's what happened," James said.

"Did you suspect something was going on between them? Ashley asked.

"Not at all, I was totally blindsided. I just thought they were good friends. You know getting drinks or going out to eat together and things like that," James said.

"James that doesn't make any sense, how could you not know something was going on if you knew your wife and spending that much time with someone else right in front of your face? How did you find out?" Ashley asked.

"That's what you would think, but let me tell you the rest of the story. One Wednesday I called Shenita and told her I would at the office about two hours late putting together a presentation for a prospect I had been working on bringing in for about six months that was coming into the office the next day. Shenita said she understood and usually went to the gym after work on Wednesdays anyway. At the last minute something came up and the appointment cancelled and rescheduled. I decided to surprise Shenita and got one of her favorite take-out meals, some wine and have it waiting on her when she got home. Well I was the one that was in for a surprise. I walked into the house and heard noises coming from the bedroom. When I opened the bedroom door, there she was naked, on her back with her exercise instructor's face buried between her legs. Shenita didn't even notice me standing there at first and then she opened her eyes and had a look of panic on her face. For the first time in my life I felt like really physically hurting somebody, but I kept my head about myself. I let her so-called friend leave my house without violence because my wife was the one that promised before God to be faithful to me," James said.

"Oh my God! You caught her in the act with another man in your house?! James, that's awful.

I'm so sorry," Ashley said with a pained look on her face.

"Ashley, that was part of the problem. Her exercise instructor's name was Kendra. She was a woman," James said with a pained expression on his face.

"A woman! Your wife had an affair with another woman?! I mean, but that would mean she…" Ashley said before James cut her off.

"That she was gay or bisexual. Yes, but she said she wasn't sure, but she told me they formed an emotional connection that became physical. Ashley, Shenita said we could work it out, because what she had with Kendra was totally different than what she had with me! Can you believe that? Kendra had been to our house before for dinner. I thought they were just friends. I never suspected that my wife was having an affair with another woman. Ashley, she brought that bitch to my house and into my bed! I couldn't deal with it and we decide the best thing was to go our separate ways so she could figure out who she was and for me, the trust was gone," James said while standing and looking out over the horizon.

"James, I'm so sorry," Ashley said while touching James on his shoulder.

"It was rough. I felt helpless. It was like a total rejection of me, not just as her husband, but as a man. I couldn't give her what that woman could, no matter what I did. I felt useless and like I wasn't much of a man to let a woman take my wife from me," James said.

"James, you weren't the problem. She had something inside her that other woman saw and brought to the surface. I know of a woman that left her husband for another woman after they had three children and fifteen years of marriage. She discovered who she really was after all that time," Ashley said.

"Maybe you're right. You're the first person I've really told the whole story too. I was too embarrassed to let anyone else in on all the details. I just told them we were growing in different directions and decided to end things before we had children and got them involved in our mess. We were going in different directions all right. I've always felt like I could tell you anything, you know, with our past together," James said.

"Of course you can. I mean it's been a long time, but we used to share everything," Ashley said.

"Well, that's my sad relationship story, what about you?" James asked.

Ashley went on to tell James about her latest adventure with Jerome.

"Wait a minute. You were getting your freak on when his fiancée, that you didn't know existed, walked in on you and pulled out a gun! Wow!" James said while shaking his head.

"I mean, I was in shock. I didn't know who she was. Jerome lied to me about everything to get what he wanted. I guess I was just another piece of ass to him," Ashley said.

"What did she do?" James asked.

"She wasn't angry at me because she figured out he had lied to me about everything. She left and told him to get out and be gone by the time she got back. I was so pissed and felt like a fool. I took a couple of days off and went to visit my folks to get away and clear my head," Ashley informed.

"It looks like we both have hit some rough patches in the relationship department since we left college," James said as he hung his head.

"James, I'm so tired of lies and bullshit. Guys will say anything to get in a woman's panties, knowing all the time they don't mean it. Most of the times the women know they're lying, but still play along with their stupid games. I'm just tired of it. I'm ready for a serious man and relationship," Ashley said.

James looked out across the patio and Ashley stood alongside him staring at the lights in the distance since the sun had disappeared below the horizon. As they stood next to each other James reached over and took Ashley's hand in his and she did not object. Ashley swallowed hard with her heart pounding in her chest before James turned and faced her. James bent down and kissed Ashley lightly on the lips.

"James, it's been a long time…" Ashley said before being cut off by a more forceful kiss.

Ashley responded in kind.

"I never stopped thinking about you Ashley," James said as he kissed Ashley again.

"Oh James," Ashley responded in kind.

James knew what Ashley liked or at least what she responded to in the past as he ran his hands over her top that covered her heaving mounds of flesh. James deftly unbuttoned Ashley top and freed her braless breasts. James always loved Ashley's grapefruit sized orbs since he could almost take one of them entirely into his mouth at once and finally he tasted one of his favorite fruits again after years of deprivation. Ashley was breathing heavily and she reached her right hand inside the waistband of James' shorts, grasped his stiffening manhood and remembered her favorite instrument of pleasure from the distant past. Ashley was feeling a sexual urgency she hadn't felt in years as she was on fire inside. James sensed Ashley's desire and turned her around so that her back was facing him. Ashley placed her hands on the glass of the patio door while James pulled her shorts down to her ankles and she stepped out of them. James had removed his shorts and saw Ashley push her ass out toward him while resting her weight on her hands braced against the door's glass. There was no time for formalities or foreplay because eight years of separation was coming to a swift end. Ashley elevated her ass by standing on the tip of her toes and she felt James large hands grab her by the waist. After eight years of separation, closing those final few inches separating their bodies seem to take forever. Then she felt James' intimate touch once more and Ashley's mouth opened in a gasp at the sensation of James going where he had not been in eight years.

"Oh James!" Ashley exclaimed as he literally lifted her body off the floor with his initial forward thrust.

James moved Ashley's body forward until her naked flesh was pressed up against the glass of the door. Ashley's face was turned to one side and her breath condensed on the outside of the inner panel of the double paned glass. Ashley's face, breasts and torso were pressed against the glass as James thrust forcefully into her molten womanhood from behind.

"That's it! Fuck me James like you used to with that big black dick baby!" Ashley urged.

"Ashley, I missed you so much. Oh baby, I'm about to come," James uttered after several minutes.

That was not some gentle reunion of long lost lovers, but an urgent intimate and physical encounter to erase years of longing from being apart. Suddenly, Ashley pushed back from the glass and dropped to her knees in front of James. The outline of Ashley's torso was still visible on the glass although she had moved on to other pursuits.

"Give that big dick to me baby!" Ashley said as she engulfed James with her mouth.

Ashley worked her magic to receive James' energy and get what she had missed for years.

"Uhhh! Uhhh!" James said as he held the back of Ashley's head as he released more than just his pent up sexual tensions.

James also released a good measure of the pain he had held onto from his failed marriage and wounded pride. Ashley then pulled her head back and took a huge gulp of air.

"Ahh!" Ashley exclaimed as she inhaled and literally released James from her oral embrace.

James was temporarily spent and lifted Ashley to her feet and kissed her as deeply as he could.

"What was that?" James asked.

"I wanted to show you that you are all the man a woman can handle and need. Spend the night with me and we can see what else we've learned over eight years. I've missed you so much," Ashley said.

"I've missed you too and that's an offer I can't resist," James said as he picked Ashley up, carried her to the sofa and positioned her on her hands and knees.

James knelt behind Ashley and used his tongue to drive her into a sexual frenzy. James didn't miss lavishing attention on a single inch of Ashley's rear and probed areas no man had previously. Ashley then felt something new that surprised her and it wasn't from James's tongue.

"Oh! James is that your finger? Are you sticking your finger in there? Ohh, damn. That's my asshole baby! Take it easy," Ashley said.

James continued his attention to her once virgin passage and what initially felt strange began to feel pleasant.

"Does that feel good to you baby?" James asked.

"Yes. It feels different, but good," Ashley replied with her head resting on her arms on the back of the sofa.

Ashley then felt something very different after she had become accustomed to what James was doing to her once forbidden passage with his fingers.

"Oh baby! Damn James! That's not your finger. That's your cock! Oh shit!" Ashley said as her eyes opened wide.

Beads of sweat popped out on Ashley's forehead as she held onto the back of the sofa as

James made his way into new territory for both of them.

"You're in my ass baby! Fuck!" Ashley exclaimed with her eyes as wide as they could get.

They both paused. James started slowly and then Ashley began to meet his rhythm as she pressed her body backwards to enhance a new sensation.

"Goddamn James! Yes, baby that's it. You're in my ass! Fuck my ass baby!" Ashley encouraged.

Ashley reached her right hand back under her body and aided James efforts with some self-stimulation of her own. Combined with the erotic thoughts and sensations of what James was doing to her body and what she added with her own efforts, Ashley felt like she experienced an explosion of sexual sensations that coursed throughout her body.

"Oh shit! Ungh!" Ashley exclaimed as her entire body shook and trembled in ecstasy.

James collapsed on top of Ashley on the sofa as they were both totally exhausted by the torrid reigniting of their sexual passion. Ashley and James finally fell asleep on the sofa after making up for eight years of being apart and showing each other everything they had experienced of a carnal nature during that time span. Ashley woke up the next morning with James embracing her in a spoon position. Ashley turned her head and kissed James on the lips.

"James, last night was awesome. I guess you could say you finally turned me out after all this time, but what do we do now? Ashley said.

"Well we know the sex is still hot. I guess we need to find out if we still have that emotional fire inside for each other. It's been a long time, but I want to give it a chance if you do," James said.

"I do. I want to try and see if we can reconnect and get that feeling back like we had before. You were so damn bad last night. I can't believe I let you fuck me in the ass. I've never done that before, but it was so hot and tight. I think I need to go to church after that," Ashley said as she kissed James.

"Go to church! Ashley, you're still crazy," James said with a laugh.

5

Ashley started the next week with a new outlook on life and a smile on her face that didn't go unnoticed by her coworkers, especially Janeka. Janeka was about to walk by Ashley's office when she looked in and saw Ashley with her chin in her hand while gazing out of her window with a smile on her face. Janeka stepped inside Ashley's office.

"Hello, earth to Ashley," Janeka said.

Ashley, who seemed slightly startled, sat up in her chair.

"Oh, hi Janeka, I didn't notice you standing there," Ashley said.

"You didn't notice me standing here for fifteen seconds. What's going on with you, just sitting there smiling and spaced out? Did something happen over the weekend?" Janeka asked as she closed Ashley's office door.

"I spent some time getting reacquainted with James and that's about it," Ashley said.

"James? Oh, your old college friend you were meeting. You said he was married. Ashley, don't tell me you fucked that married man!" Janeka said.

"Shhh, keep your voice down. You know these office walls are made of nothing but those same thin panels that the cubicles are made of. I don't want the other managers all in my personal business," Ashley said.

"Oops, sorry," Janeka said.

"James got a divorce a couple of years ago. I didn't know that until we met for dinner Friday night. I invited him over to my house Saturday since he didn't have any plans for the weekend and you know..." Ashley said before Janeka completed her sentence.

"One thing led to another," Janeka said with a wink.

"Yes it did, asshole," Ashley replied with a smile.

"So what was better, the one thing or the other?" Janeka asked.

"They were both great," Ashley answered.

"So Miss, do you need to see a chiropractor?" Janeka asked.

"Yes, I need to get my back adjusted because he knocked it out," Ashley answered.

"Good job," Janeka said as she gave Ashley a fist bump.

"You are so silly. See you later," Ashley said as Janeka left her office.

Ashley and James rekindled their relationship that was interrupted by years, distance and a failed marriage. Ashley found that James had changed and felt he had lost some of his natural trust and optimism due to how his marriage came apart. James discovered that Ashley was a worldlier woman than he remembered from their college days when she was fresh from a small rural town. Overall they both liked the more seasoned versions of each other and began to feel emotional embers they thought were long extinguished flicker with a faint glow.

Two months after James moved to Dallas he was settled in. James bought a home with four bedrooms, three bathrooms and a pool in a gated community. James was anxious to show his new place to Ashley and was picking her up on a sunny Saturday afternoon. James called when he was downstairs and Ashley came down to meet him. Ashley was looking around for James' SUV when a black sports car pulled up next to her. Ashley looked over at the car and the passenger door swung open next to her.

"Get in!" a man said from inside.

Ashley bent down and looked inside and James was in the driver's seat.

"James, what are you doing in this?!" Ashley asked as she managed to maneuver her body into the passenger seat without showing too much in her short skirt.

"This is mine," James said as he sped off.

"Oh my God! Is this a Corvette?" Ashley asked.

"Yes. A new Corvette Z06. I've wanted one for two years. It's loud, fast and American made," James said.

"When I was in high school, all the guys wanted one. Well the Black guys did. The White guys wanted dually pickup trucks. I love this, but it only has two seats," Ashley said.

"I know. One for you and one for me, if you want to be my ride-or-die chick," James said.

"Yes, I'll be your ride-or-die chick," Ashley said as James entered the 161 toll road.

James saw an open stretch of pavement ahead. James pressed down on the throttle and Ashley was slammed back into her seat and her eyes became as big as saucers as the engine screamed along with her. As the digital speedometer touched one hundred and forty miles per hour, James took his foot off the gas and slowed so he could exit to go to his new home.

"Oh my God James! Are you crazy?! I can hardly breathe. My whole body is tingling," Ashley said.

James drove into the garage at his home and gave Ashley the grand tour. After a change of clothes, they went out back to the swimming pool and got in the spa. Once they had consumed several glasses of wine, James turned the lights off and removed Ashley's swimsuit and his shorts. The couple sat in the bubbling water sipping wine in the darkness.

"James did you ever think you would be living like this considering where you came from?" Ashley asked.

"No way, I felt like I was lucky to come out of my neighborhood alive. Quite a few of my friends that I grew up with are gone now. Some are dead. A lot of them are in prison and drugs have some of them strung out so bad that they may as well be in prison or dead. When I went to college I was just happy to get away from home. I didn't know anything about the business world. I didn't think a black man was allowed to live this way," James said.

"What do you mean by allowed to live this way?" Ashley asked.

"I mean, I knew some Black entertainers and famous athletes lived in luxury, but not a regular Black man like me. I didn't have any special talent, so I couldn't even imagine living any better than the way I grew up. That's why I busted my ass so hard when I got to New York. Failing was not an option. What about you? You're living in a high-rise condo looking out over the big city," James asked.

"There's no way I could have even imagined this when I was young. I grew up in that old trailer house. The other White kids called me White trash. I didn't know what was going to happen to me and then I got that call from the Dean of the Business School telling me I scored high enough on a national test to go to college and it was paid for. Man, I was ready to go, but didn't even know what it really meant for my future. If someone would have told me when I was in high school that I would have an important corporate job and live in the city like I'm doing, I would have told them they were crazy, but it's real. Sometimes I get scared that it might all disappear and I will end up back on the bottom where I came from," Ashley admitted.

"That won't happen. You're too smart, too talented and too sexy to fail," James said.

"James, what does sexy have to do with anything?" Ashley asked.

"That's very important to me," James said as he pulled Ashley to face him in the spa.

Ashley floated into James' arms as he sat on the second of three steps on the side of the spa. As Ashley placed her arms around James' neck she kissed him and he caressed her firm ass cheeks. Ashley slowly sat on James lap and wrapped her legs around his waist.

"Can you feel me inside you Ashley?" James asked.

"Yes baby, I feel you," Ashley said as she began to move her hips in an undulating motion.

"I could stay this way forever with you Ashley. Ashley, I love you," James said.

"You do? James, I've wanted to hear that again for eight years. I should have gone to New York with you when you asked me. I would never hurt you like she did because I love you too much," Ashley said with tears streaming down her face.

The two lovers completed their carnal dance in the darkness of a fall night under the Texas sky.

Ashley and Jamie's relationship had been confined to interactions between just the two of them together, but that was about to change due to a company recognition trip that Ashley was rewarded with due to the success of the winter marketing campaign. Ashley could invite a guest to come with her and she asked James if he want to be her guest. The trip was a four day affair in Hawaii, that began on a Thursday and ended on the following Sunday.

"Do you want to go?" Ashley asked.

"Yeah, I think I can make it. It's two months out so I can arrange for someone to be acting manager while I'm out. Go ahead and turn my name in. Is everything good over there with you as far as me going?" James asked.

"Yeah, but it will confirm my status as one of them. You know it's been my reputation as one of those White women that only dates Black guys, so you being my guest will settle that as a confirmed fact," Ashley said.

"So you turned a few your White coworkers down, so how did it come to their attention that they were not your type?" James asked.

"One of them asked my friend, Janeka to put in a good word for him and she casually informed him that I only went out with Black guys. I think it stunned them because there was nothing they could do about it. They couldn't become Black men. It's not like I'm the only woman in the world, but it didn't sit well with them. Rejection for something like that must suck," Ashley said.

"Yes it does," James said.

"Oh James, I'm sorry. I wasn't thinking about how your wife. Never mind, I'm sorry," Ashley said.

"It's no big deal. We're together now and that's all that matters," James said.

"That is all that matters, isn't it," Ashley agreed.

It was settled and James would accompany Ashley on her company trip to Hawaii, but there was another trip James was taking with Ashley that had them a little worried. James would go with Ashley on a trip to visit her parents the next weekend. Ashley thought it was time for James to meet her parents since they were officially an exclusive couple. This trip would confirm if her father really meant he understood and respected her choices in men. Ashley was a little concerned, but understood it was her life, but preferred for her family to be supportive of her if she was happy with James.

6

Ashley never knew a week at work could go by so fast and before she realized it she was in the passenger seat of James' Corvette as they cruised down Interstate 45 toward Galveston, TX.

"Are you okay?" James asked when he glanced over at Ashley.

"I'm a little nervous about my dad. He said he understood, but you know, he still sees me as being sixteen or something," Ashley said.

"You don't have to explain. I grew up in Shreveport and even though everyone went to school and worked together, a lot of us still lived in neighborhoods that were almost all Black or all White. Let's not even talk about church on Sundays, everybody pretty much worshiped with their own kind. We still get the side eye when we go out together in a city like Dallas, so I understand where your dad is coming from," James said.

Before they knew it they were crossing the bridge to enter Galveston.

"Take the next right and turn into the driveway with the blue mailbox," Ashley said.

James followed Ashley's directions and parked in from of the relatively small white home.

"Ashley, you made it!" her mother said as she came outside.

"Hi mom," Ashley said as she hugged her mother.

"Mom this is my boyfriend, James," Ashley said.

"Hello James. I'm Ashley's mother, Katherine, nice to meet you," James said.

"Nice to meet you again, we met a long time ago when you came to Florida for Ashley's graduation," James reminded.

"I remember that, but that was eight years ago. There must be a story behind how you two ended up back together. Come on inside," Katherine said.

"Where's dad?" Ashley asked.

"He'll be back soon. He went to get some crabs. I'm making gumbo for dinner," Katherine said.

"I love gumbo," James said.

"Well, it took me awhile, but my neighbor taught me how to cook it. I never cooked that kind of food in Lufkin before we moved here," Katherine said.

Everyone went inside and sat in the living room when they heard the front door open.

"Hey, who's driving the fancy car outside?" Edward said as he walking in carrying a shopping bag that Katherine took from him.

"Hi dad!" Ashley said as she stood and hugged Edward.

"Hello honey," Edward said.

"Dad, this is James," Ashley said.

"Hello James, wait a minute, aren't you the same guy…" Edward said before James finished his thought.

"The same guy you met in Florida. Yes sir, I'm the same guy," James said.

"Well all I can say, Is you knew a good thing when you saw it and came back," Edward said.

"Dad, you're embarrassing me," Ashley said with her cheeks turning red.

"It's true. You're one in a million," Edward said to Ashley who smiled.

"So that's your hot rod out there. You know I meant to bring back a bottle of wine for dinner. James, would you mind driving me down to the store?" Edward asked.

"No, I wouldn't mind at all. Ashley we'll be back," James said.

Ashley had a concerned look on her face.

"Okay, be careful," Ashley said.

James and Edward left the house and drove away.

"Mom, what's that all about? Dad doesn't drink wine," Ashley said.

"Well you know your father. You've never brought a man over to meet us before, so you must be serious about him. Your father is just doing what fathers do. He wants to make sure James is serious, wants the best for you and will treat you right," Katherine said.

"Mom, I'm a grown woman living on my own," Ashley reminded.

"Ashley, to us, you're never grown. You're our little girl. You'll understand one day if you ever give me some grandchildren," Katherine said.

After a while Ashley began to worry.

"They've been gone for an hour. What's taking so long," Ashley said to her mother when she heard James car pull into the driveway.

James and her father were laughing when they walked inside.

"Katherine, we need to get one of those cars. I tell you that thing makes me feel like I did when I was young and crazy. Remember when I souped up my dad's old Ford pickup. Man that was fun," Edward said.

"So where did you guys go? The store is just around the corner," Ashley questioned.

"My my, Miss nosey, I wasn't going to let him get in trouble. We just toured around a little and talked. I showed James some of the sights around town, but you better be on your toes, Missy, every time we stopped people were staring. Two girls walked by and were just smiling and waving at us. I figured they must have been interested in me," Edward said.

"Very funny dad," Ashley said.

"We just talked. James is a good man. I know how to determine if a man is a straight shooter," Edward said.

"Thank you, Mr. Riley," James said.

"Don't let that go to your head James. There's not much room in that car already," Ashley said as she walked back to the kitchen.

"She's feisty today. Let's leave these women alone so they can cook," James said as they went to the living room.

Ashley was shocked at how well her parents were reacting to James as her boyfriend. When it got later in the day, Ashley brought up getting a hotel room for the night.

"A hotel room, that's nonsense. We have two empty bedrooms. Now I don't care what you two do back in Dallas, but Ashley you can sleep in one room and James you can sleep in the other one. You're not married so, there won't be any playing house under my roof," Katherine said.

"Mom, really?" Ashley commented.

"No that's fine and I understand where you're coming from. My mother doesn't go for that kind of thing either. Your house, your rules," James said.

Ashley gave James a look like she couldn't believe what she was hearing. A few hours later Ashley said she was going to bed and took the bedroom on the right side of the hallway. James and Edward stayed up a couple of hours later discussing the playoff prospects of the Dallas and Houston professional football teams respectively.

James went to his room and occupied himself by surfing the internet on his mobile phone. Around one o'clock in the morning, James opened the door to his room and stuck his head into the hallway. James heard three distinct snoring sounds coming from different rooms. Ashley's parents slept in a bedroom near the front of the house close to the kitchen and he could hear sounds of their deep sleep. James took one careful step across the hallway and slowly twisted the door knob to Ashley's bedroom door and to his delight it was not locked. James tip toed his way to the foot of her bed aided by the moonlight shining through a decorative semicircular window above the primary windows in the room. Ashley was lying on her back sound asleep. James knelt at the foot of the bed, lifted the sheets and carefully maneuvered his body upward. James carefully used his hands to gently push Ashley's legs apart. Ashley was not wearing panties under her nightgown and James placed a soft kiss on her exposed womanhood. Ashley rolled her head to one side and James then used his tongue to taste her sweet nectar. Ashley then turned her head to the opposite side from the direction it was facing. James then treated Ashley's private parts like his favorite piece of hard candy that he was trying to lick away the hard outer coating to reach the soft and sweet substance in the middle.

Ashley thought she was having the most vivid wet dream in her life when she reached her hands down and felt James' head with his closely cut hair. When she opened her eyes, Ashley realized she was in the same bedroom in her parent's house that she went to sleep in earlier that night, but she was no longer alone.

"It's me," James whispered from under the sheets.

"It had better be you. What are you doing in here?" Ashley said in a frantic hushed tone.

"Can't you tell?" James said as Ashley clamped her legs together tightly.

James climbed upon on top of Ashley's body until he was face to face with her.

"James, we could get caught and my dad would freak out if he found you in here," Ashley said.

"I don't think he's going to wake up. We had quite a few drinks. He was feeling no pain by the time he went to bed," James informed quietly.

"You got my dad drunk?" Ashley questioned.

"No, just feeling real good," James informed.

Ashley's resistance was growing weaker as James was constantly pressing his case by alternatively kissing and nibbling on his favorite fruit.

"James, baby, I can't do it in my parent's house," Ashley said without much resolve.

"While James was lavishing attention on Ashley's breasts with his oral ministrations, he allowed his right hand to wander down to the valley between her thighs. Once James' fingers attempted to pry open her clasped thighs, Ashley relented and relaxed her muscles and allowed him free access. Before long Ashley whispered a crucial question into James' ear.

"Did you lock the door to my room?" Ashley asked while breathing heavy.

"Yes," James' answered.

"Come on baby, but we have to be quiet," Ashley said as she shifted her body downward on the mattress under James' body.

Ashley welcomed James with an intimate embrace and released a silent gasp as he joined with her body. Of all the times they had been together, Ashley felt more aroused than at any other time she could recall, because there she was breaking the ultimate taboo by engaging in hot, steamy and lustful relations with a Black man under her father's roof. She dared not utter a sound as this beautiful, chocolate skin toned man that she loved drove into the core of her being with his bronze staff. If she could have screamed it would have been primal, but for Ashley being forced to contain her ecstasy internally increased the intensity. Least creaky mattress springs betrayed them, Ashley and James confined they movements to maximum contact between their bodies with minimum motion of the bed supporting them. There they were engaged in a prolonged and slow grinding of their intertwined bodies bathed in soft moonlight.

Ashley felt a dam of emotion and bliss build up inside her to the point of overflowing, but she knew screaming out was not an option. Instead of vocalizing when her dam burst, Ashley stuffed the corner of the pillow she was lying on into her mouth and bit down hard onto it while she trembled in release. James felt the sensations of his lover and soon followed in kind with a sensation that seemed to come from a place he had not experienced before. The lovers were still locked in a perspiration soaked embrace as they panted from their previous exertion. Slowly, James' disengaged from Ashley and rolled onto his back alongside her.

"James, I think you should go to your room before we get caught," Ashley suggested in hushed tones.

"Okay, I think your right," James said as he sat up on the edge of the mattress.

Ashley reached out and rubbed her hand down James sweaty back.

"James, that was the best ever. I love you," Ashley said.

"Yes it was. I love you too Ashley," James said as he made his way across the hallway to his room.

As Ashley looked up at the ceiling in the darkness, she realized something she was afraid to acknowledge to herself previously. Ashley realized she craved the additional excitement of being with a Black man. Although she was not sexually promiscuous and preferred to be in a monogamous relationship, a part of her felt like she was cheating, not on her lover but on her race and heritage even when she was with the man she loved. A strange type of guilt washed over Ashley and she knew she needed to address it with James because it was gnawing at her and would not subside.

The next day as they all ate breakfast before James and Ashley headed back to Dallas, it was evident that James had won over Edward and gained his approval as a suitable boyfriend for his daughter. Later they all said their goodbyes. James and Ashley drove away with her parents looking on as James' vehicle made a right turn and disappeared from view. After James and Ashley were gone for an hour, Katherine went into the room Ashley slept in to change the sheets. Katherine pulled the top sheet down and immediately saw tell-tale stains left behind by James and Ashley from the night before.

"That little hot ass hard headed little girl," Katherine mumbled as she removed all of the bed covers.

Katherine washed Ashley's evidence out of the sheets and never mentioned anything to Edward about it.

On the way back to Dallas, Ashley brought up something that had been on her mind since she made love to James the night before.

"James, I've got something to tell you," Ashley said.

"Okay, what is it?" James asked.

"Something has been bothering me since we were together last night. I realized something about how I feel when I'm with you that way and I'm not sure how you feel about it," Ashley said.

"Okay, I'm starting to get worried about what you're going to say. Did you realize you don't love me or something?" James asked.

"Oh no, it's nothing like that, because I do love you and that's the thing. Last night I realized I love making love to you, but at the same time in my mind I sometimes had this feeling that I was, you know, breaking some sacred rule by having forbidden sex with a Black man," Ashley admitted.

"What? Ashley I'm one guy. You were making love to me and I happen to be a Black man. Am I missing something here?" James asked.

"I know, but sometimes I opened my eyes and saw your dark skin against mine and it made everything more exciting to know that I was doing something a lot of White people hate more than anything else they can think of. I realized I got an extra charge when I thought of the fact that I was having taboo sex with a Black man. Does that make you angry or feel strange in any way?" Ashley asked.

"Let me ask you something. When you see other Black men you don't know, do you think about what it would be like to be with them, you know as a forbidden partner?" James asked.

"No. I don't know or have any feelings for those men. I only think about that sometimes when we're having sex," Ashley said.

"Well it really just sounds like a little fantasizing to me that makes our sex life more exciting, but it also seems like you have some feelings deep inside about Whites and Blacks being together romantically," James said.

"You know, where I grew up there were a lot of White men that would kill a Black man for having sex with their daughters or sisters, even if it was consensual. I grew up understanding that, even though I went out with a few Black guys in high school. I knew by doing that I would be seen in a certain way as somehow disgracing my race. I knew that was stupid because we are all the same inside. I mean, do you sometimes think of me differently as a White woman when we are together," Ashley asked.

"Do you mean when I say things like give me that White pussy or ride this big Black dick," James said with a laugh.

"You do say those things sometimes, don't you?" Ashley said.

"Ashley look, we have such a complicated racial history in the United States that we over analyze everything. We love each other, right, so if you like to think of me as your secret Black lover to get you more revved up when we're together, that's okay," James said.

"Okay. I don't know why that bothered me so much. Well I guess I do. I didn't want you to think I was disrespecting you by thinking that way when we are making love. It almost felt like I was cheating on you," Ashley said.

"Look, if you want to cheat on me with me, I'm okay with it. Ashley, I'm just joking. I understand what you mean. It's about being present and honest when we are with each other, but we can still have a little fun," James said.

"Okay, I was afraid you would think I was crazy for thinking what I did, but we have a deal. I can be the White woman you're fucking twice a week behind the barn without anyone knowing about it. That kind of stuff did go one when I was growing up, I heard about it," Ashley said.

"Oh, that's hot," James said as they both laughed.

7

Ashley and James transitioned into a new phase in their relationship. Almost every weekend Ashley or James would stay at one or the other's home and they spent as much time together as possible. When the morning came for them to embark on Ashley's company trip to Hawaii they left from James' house because it was closer to the airport. Once at the airport, James and Ashley made their way to a gathering area her company had set up as a reception room. Ashley walked into the room to curious onlookers that were getting their first sighting of her with James.

"Hey girl," Janeka said as she hugged Ashley.

"Hi Janeka. Janeka this is my boyfriend James. James this is my friend Janeka that I told you about," Ashley said as she introduced them.

"Hi James, it's good to finally meet you. I've heard a lot about you from Ashley, but somehow she hasn't invited me over to meet you, have you Ashley?" Janeka said.

"I've been so busy that it just kept slipping my mind," Ashley said.

"Yeah, right," Janeka said as a handsome Black man walked up to Janeka and gave her a drink in a glass.

"Oh, Ashley, this is my friend Kevon. He's going on the trip with me," Janeka said.

"Nice to meet you Kevon. Jeneka has told me nothing about you, have you Jeneka?" Ashley said.

Kevon and James introduced themselves to each other.

"Kevon and I have only been seeing each other for a couple of months, so I thought I would wait a little while before telling other people about us," Janeka said.

"I get it. Hey it looks like it's time to go to our gate for boarding," Ashley said when the group began to move toward the door.

An announcement was made to proceed to the boarding gate and everyone moved in that direction. In short order everyone was seated and the airliner was moving down the runway for the over eight hour flight to Hawaii. The flight was as uneventful as it was long. Finally after losing five hours in time zone shift the group landed in Hawaii. Once at the hotel Ashley and Janeka booked rooms next to each other so it would be easier when they decided to get together for dinner or lunch. Once in their room, Ashley and James stepped out onto their room's twenty-ninth floor balcony and looked out over the Pacific Ocean. James wrapped his arms around Ashley and when they turned to their right,

Janeka and Kevon were standing on their balcony also.

"Howdy neighbor," Janeka said and they all shared a laugh.

"Hey guys. I guess we'll get ready for the opening business meeting tonight. See you there," Ashley said as they all went inside.

A few hours later Ashley and James went downstairs to the conference room that was set up for a dinner meeting, presentation and live entertainment. Ashley spotted Janeka and Kevon sitting at one of the round table and sat beside them. After a couple of welcome speeches from the company president everyone enjoyed a three course meal while a renowned singer performed some of her greatest hits for the assembled group. It was only eight o'clock local time in Hawaii, but the five hour time difference had caught up to everyone and many were nodding at their tables since their biological clocks were still on United States mainland time. Their bodies felt like it was in the early morning of the next day. When the last song was finished the group was dismissed so they could catch up on much needed sleep. Before everyone left, Ashley pulled Janeka aside so she could ask her a question.

"Where did you meet Kevon?" Ashley asked.

"The last place I expected to meet a man, at church. I went to a christening for my friend Shemeka's baby at her church and saw him and thought he was cute. I didn't know he liked what he saw too. He knew Shemeka and gave her his number to give to me. Shemeka said he was a good guy, so I called him and here we are," Janeka said with a smile.

"Congratulations. Well I'm going to bed before I go to sleep standing up. See you later," Ashley said.

Once they were back in their hotel room Ashley and James were almost asleep before their heads hit the pillows, but as often happens their bodies woke up on their old time back home and it was three o'clock in the morning and still dark outside.

"Are you awake," James asked.

"Yes, I've just been lying here trying not to wake you up," Ashley said.

"What was that?" James said when he heard a noise.

"Ohh shit!" Ashley and James heard faintly from a woman's voice through the wall.

Ashley and James looked at each other in the near darkness. Then a clear thumping noise could be heard on the other side of the wall.

"Fuck me Kevon!" came through loud enough to be heard from the next room.

"That's it bitch! Take this dick baby!" a man's voice said.

"Ughn! Ughn!" were the final utterances Ashley and James heard from next door.

Ashley and James realized they had just heard Janeka having sex with Kevon and figured they thought no one else would be awake at that time of morning to hear them. It didn't take much to give Ashley and James a similar motivation although they practiced the method employed when they were at her parents' house to avoid detection by their next door neighbors. Ashley clung to James' body and she gasped in silence as she experienced bliss in paradise.

On the third day of the trip Ashley and James were hiking up a mountainous trail through a rain forest with waterfalls on one side and lush tropical vegetation on the other side when James stopped. There was no one else around at the time.

"Hold up, I need to stop and tighten my shoelaces," James said as they both stopped.

James knelt and unnoticed by Ashley he slipped his right hand into the pocket of his shorts. Ashley was looking around and when she turned she saw James holding a box. Ashley's eyes grew wide in surprise. James took Ashley's left hand and held it and opened the box that contained a ring with sparkling diamonds all around it. Ashley felt like she was about to pass out and a small crowd of hikers had stopped to witness what was taking place.

"Ashley, we were apart for years, but we found each other again. I can't imagine my life without you and don't want to take that chance. Ashley, will you marry me and make me the happiest man alive?" James asked.

"Ashley took her right hand from over her mouth and said one word.

"Yes!" Ashley said.

After slipping the engagement ring on the fourth finger of Ashley's left hand, James stood, embraced his new fiancée and kissed her. The people around them applauded and gave their congratulations. Ashley and James both had tears running down their faces. Ashley stared at her hand in disbelief.

"When did you decide this? I can't believe it," Ashley said.

"I decided I wanted to marry you before we went to your parents' house. I asked your father for his blessings to marry you when we went on that drive. It wasn't all smiles like you saw when we came back to the house. We had quite argument. He said he couldn't see his only daughter being married to a Black man and didn't think it was natural, but I told him I loved you and you loved me. I asked him what was more important, his happiness or yours. I told him I was asking for his blessings, but not his permission. For some reason he calmed down and told me if I really loved you and you loved me, then we had his blessings because it was your life and he didn't want to do anything to drive you away from him," James said.

"James, you fought for us. I love you even more now. I'm going to be the best wife I can be to you," Ashley said.

Ashley looked around and didn't see anyone, grabbed James hand and led him into the thick vegetation.

"What are you doing?" James asked.

"Keep your voice down," Ashley whispered.

Ashley pulled her shorts down and braced herself against the trunk of a tree with her naked ass sticking out toward James. James didn't need any additional instructions as he dropped his shorts down to his ankles also. James grabbed Ashley by the waist and sunk into Ashley's molten core. James and Ashley consummated their engagement in the middle of nature's glory before quickly pulling their hiking shorts back up and continuing along their way as if nothing ever happened.

Before the last business meeting of their trip to Hawaii, Janeka walked up to Ashley and saw something new on her finger.

"Ashley, what is that on your finger? No he didn't!" Janeka said.

"Yes he did. We're getting married!" Ashley said and hugged Janeka as they jumped around.

"Oh my God! Congratulations!" Janeka said.

Ashley told Janeka how surprised she was and how James proposed to her.

"How have things been going with Kevon?" Ashley asked.

"It's been great. I'm keeping my fingers crossed," Janeka said.

"Things must be going well from what I heard that first night, I think you need a chiropractor," Ashley said.

"What are you talking about? Oh my God! You heard us?!" Janeka said with a look of embarrassment on her face.

"Yes, I heard you getting your freak on," Ashley said.

"Girl it was good too. I'm not complaining," Janeka said with a smile.

"Well, I'm happy you found a good man," Ashley said.

Ashley and Janeka went to the meeting and the next day they all flew out of Hawaii and back to reality back home. On the trip back Ashley felt like she was flying higher than the aircraft taking her back to the mainland. Ashley and James were basking in the afterglow of their engagement, but their joy would be short lived by news that greeted them after they arrived back home.

8

One week after their arrival back home, Ashley and James were still adjusting to being newly engaged when James got a call that turned his world upside down. James' mother, Brenda was stricken by a massive heart attack and although the paramedics were able to revive her when they arrived, she perished on the way to the emergency room. James was devastated as his father passed away when he was young and his mother was the rock he could always look to whenever he needed advice of any kind. James called Ashley and informed her of the news.

"Oh James, I'm so sorry. I know how you feel about your mother. Are you okay?" Ashley asked with tears running down her face.

"Yeah, I'm okay. I think I'm in shock or something. I feel like I'm numb. Maybe it won't hit me until I'm there and see her body. Look, I'm about to leave the office, go home and pack some things and head that way," James said.

"I'm coming with you," Ashley pronounced.

"You don't have to do that, what about your job?" James asked.

"I've worked here over eight years and have plenty of time I can take off. I love you and you're going to be my husband. I want to be there to support you through all of this," Ashley said.

"I love you and appreciate the support. How soon can you be over at my place?" James asked.

"Give me three hours and I will be there. I just have to arrange for someone to back me up here at work, swing by the house and grab some things and be right over," Ashley informed.

"Okay see you there," James said.

Three and one half hours later James and Ashley were on their way to Shreveport, Louisiana in James black Cadillac Escalade. As the miles melted away James replayed in his mind many of the experiences he had with his beloved mother over the years. James at twenty-eight years old was the youngest of four children. James had one brother, Johsua, who was five years older than he was. Joshua was a long haul trucker and owned his own big rig. Joshua lived in Memphis, Tennessee. Donita was James sister who was seven years older that he was. Donita was married to Montrell and had two children. Donita worked in an automobile manufacturing plant in South Carolina and earned a good wage, but her husband did very little to contribute to the household. James didn't care for Montrell very much and considered him to be taking advantage of his sister. Venita was James oldest sister. Venita was ten years older than James and was living in the house with James mother when she died. Venita was single and had a twenty year old daughter, Jamesha, who also lived with

James late mother along with Jamesha's three year old daughter. James loved Venita, but she seemed to harbor some resentment towards James for his success and felt that he was provided opportunities she didn't get since he was the youngest child. Venita felt her mother supported James more while she was hampered with helping with her younger siblings.

"I called and told mama we were getting married. She remembered you from graduation, but I wanted to bring you down here to meet her again, but I waited too long," James said.

"I know baby. I wish she would have been able to attend out wedding. I called my parents and told them about your mother and they sent their condolences," Ashley said.

"I appreciate that and thank them for me," James said.

The rest of James and Ashley's trip to Shreveport was uneventful until James saw all the vehicles parked around his mother's home. James then understood that this gathering was not for a family reunion or some other joyous occasion, because when he walked into that house everyone would be there except his mother. James entered the home and was greeted by his brother Joshua.

"Baby brother!" Joshua said as he embraced James.

"Joshua, how are you man?" James asked.

"Doing the best I can under the circumstances," Joshua said.

"I know man. It still hasn't hit me that mama is gone," James said.

Ashley then walked through the door.

"James you forgot your sunglasses," Ashley said.

"Well James, aren't going to introduce your older brother to this young lady?" Joshua asked.

"Ashley this is my brother Joshua. Joshua this is my fiancée Ashley," James said.

"It's nice to meet you Joshua, I just wish it wasn't under these circumstances," Ashley said as she shook Joshua's hand.

"Nice to meet you too, Ashley. Now, did James just say you were his fiancée? James did you forget to call and tell me something?" Joshua asked while looking at his brother.

"We've been engaged for only about a week and just got back from Hawaii, so it just slipped my mind," James said.

"James, it so good to see you," his sister Donita said as she came into the living room and hugged him.

"Good to see you too, sis. Ashley this is my sister Donita. Donita this is my fiancée Ashley.

"Your fiancée! It's nice to meet you Ashley, congratulations. James didn't tell me he was getting married, did you James?" Donita said.

"We just got engaged," Ashley said.

"Uncle James!" his niece Jamesha said as she walked in the door.

"Hey Jamesha," James said and embraced his niece.

"Come here Keke," James said as Jamesha's three year-old daughter hid behind her mother's legs.

"Ashley this is my niece Jamesha. Jamesha this is my fiancée Ashley," James said as he introduced them.

"Hi," Jamesha said and shook Ashley's hand.

"Where's your mother?" James asked Jamesha.

"She's outside getting groceries out of the car," Jamesha said.

"Jamesha, I see your hands are empty. Go help your mother," Donita said.

"Alright auntie, I was just bringing Keke inside, so she wouldn't be in the way," Jamesha said as she went back outside.

James also went outside and helped bring in the bags from Venita's shopping trip. Ashley's head was spinning from being introduced to everyone, but she took time out to use the bathroom. When Ashley came out of the bathroom she was looking Venita in the eyes. Venita looked Ashley up and down from head to toe.

"Who is this?" Venita turned and asked to her siblings.

"Oh my bad, Venita, this is my fiancée, Ashley. Ashley, this is my sister Venita," James said.

"It's nice to meet you Ashley," Venita said.

"It's nice to meet you too Venita," Ashley said and shook her hand.

"James, mama told me you called and said you were getting married, but obviously she didn't tell me everything," Venita said.

"Well, what all do we need to do for arrangements and I need to go to the funeral home and see mama for myself. I know you guys have seen her body since you were here before me, but I've got to see her before it really feels real to me. It still feels like she could walk through that front door at any minute," James said almost breaking down.

Venita made a move as if to console her younger brother, but Ashley went to him and embraced him as he wept.

"Oh James. It will be okay," Ashley said as he buried his head into her shoulder.

Venita looked on with her hands on her hips.

"I'm sorry ya'll, but this is just hitting me since I'm here now. I was able to hold it in before," James admitted.

"Ain't no shame man. We all loved mama," Joshua said.

"We need to go to the funeral home and make arrangements for the services and try to work something out to pay for the funeral," Venita said.

"Work something out. Didn't mama have an account set aside for this?" James asked.

"Well she did, but we can't get it. It's tied up in a loan," Venita said.

"Tied up in a loan, for what?" James asked.

"Jamesha got into a little trouble and we had to hire a lawyer to get her out of it," Venita said.

"What kind of trouble did she get into?" James asked.

"Her boyfriend was stopped while she was in the car with him and he had a lot of cocaine hidden in the trunk under the spare tire. He got busted for intent to distribute, but Jamesha didn't know anything about it. We had to hire a lawyer to defend her so she wouldn't go to prison," Venita said.

"I told that girl to stop fooling with those thugs!" James said angrily.

"I know James. I told her too," Venita said.

"Joshua, Donita, ya'll got good jobs, so together we couldn't put our mother away proper?" James asked.

"James, I haven't been on the road in six months. I had to shut it down because I got too many tickets. I've been living on my savings and ran them down. I'm getting my rig back on the road next month," Joshua informed.

"Donita, what about you and where's Montrell and your boys?" James asked.

"Montrell, is at the mall getting suits for all of them to wear to the funeral. Montrell screwed us over gambling. While I was working, he was in the casino emptying out our bank account. I almost divorced his ass, but didn't because of the boys. I was blindsided," Donita said.

"Don't worry about it. Mama had a life insurance policy I took out on her. It's in a safe deposit box at the bank she uses. I'll go get it in the morning. It's for fifty thousand, so she can be put away nice and handle any bills she might have left over. I was going to use it to take care of any bills, taxes or anything else that came along, but we'll use it to put mama away too," James said.

Ashley looked on and felt a little uncomfortable being a surprise witness to that family drama. The group went to the funeral home and James laid eyes on his mother's body for the first time. James couldn't maintain his usually calm demeanor and broke down grief-stricken. Ashley felt she made the right decision to come with James and support him during that most trying time in his life. Joshua rode with James and Ashley on the way back to his mother's house and brought up a subject that was the proverbial elephant in the room.

"James, what do we do about Venita? She's living in the house and mama's gone now. Mama made you the executor of her estate and put you over her will. Number one, she's going to be pissed about that since she's the oldest and she has nowhere else to go, so she will need to stay there, especially with her daughter and granddaughter living there too," Joshua said.

"I don't care if she stays there, but she has to pay all the bills and taxes. Mama's social security checks are gone now, so Venita has to handle everything on her own," James said.

"When do you want to do all this, you know reading the will and everything?" Joshua asked.

"I'll go by the lawyer's office tomorrow after I go to the bank. He has the latest version of the will. I need to do some shopping and when we get back we can all talk it over," James said.

"That'll work," Jerome said.

Once everyone was back at the house, they sat and decided when they would read the will. Montrell and James nephews were back at the house from their shopping trip. They also settled on sleeping arrangements. The house had three bedrooms and a sofa sleeper in the living room. Donita and Joshua brought air mattresses with them. The day was getting long and James said that he and

Ashley would sleep in the room he slept in when he was growing up.

"James, you know mama wouldn't have approved of you staying in the same room with your fiancée before you were married in her house," Venita said.

Everyone else in the house stopped in their tracks and held their breaths waiting on James' response. James turned and faced his eldest sister.

"What?! What are you talking about? Venita, I'm a grown ass man! Ashley and I are going to sleep in that room and that's the end of it!" James said.

"I know mama's gone, but at least you could show her wishes some respect and what kind of example are you setting for your nephews and niece?" Venita said.

"I'm showing mama some respect by making sure she is put away the way she would be proud of by her family. As for setting an example for my nephews and nieces, why don't you look in the mirror? You're the one that had a child out of wedlock and what did that lead too Venita? You don't get to tell me what to do. My mama is gone and you don't get to replace her. Goodnight!" James said.

"You didn't have to say that James! You didn't have to say that! Go ahead and lay down with that White hoe under your mama's roof! At least the heifer doesn't weigh four hundred pounds like most of the trailer trash White women with the black men I see around here! You don't have any respect!" Venita said angrily.

Joshua and Donita saw that things were getting out of hand and stepped in.

"Hey, hey! Venita! You're going too far now! Calm down!" Joshua said as he grabbed his sister.

"Venita, don't you talk about Ashley like that! The only reason I'm not over there beating your ass is because you're my sister! We're going to bed and you need think about how you showed your ass tonight! Let's go Ashley!" James said as he grabbed Ashley by the hand and slammed the bedroom door.

Ashley was stunned by the events of the night, but she knew better than to get in the middle of family issues at sensitive time like the death of the matriarch. Hearing her future sister-in-law call her a White whore shook Ashley to her foundation. Ashley was tired, but found she was wide awake looking up at the ceiling in the darkness.

"Are you awake?" Ashley asked.

"Yeah, I can't sleep," James said.

"What happened out there tonight?" Ashley asked softly.

"Venita's years of frustration over the results of her bad life decisions just exploded. I'm

94

sorry for what Venita said about you. Everything about tonight was ugly," James said.

"James, what you said to Venita, that really hurt her. I could tell," Ashley said.

"I know it did. I just reacted and went for the kill. We can't fall apart as a family because our mother died. Hopefully we can work things out," James said.

Ashley and James finally went to sleep. Early the next day Ashley opened her eyes and the smell of bacon hit her nostrils. James was still snoring next to her. Ashley knew bathroom access would be difficult with so many people in a house with one bathroom. Grabbing her clothes and toiletry bag, Ashley walked to the bathroom door and got lucky as James' niece, Jamesha, was exiting. Ashley went into the bathroom, showered, refreshed herself and put on fresh clothes. Ashley exited the bathroom and headed back to the bedroom where James was still sleeping. To avoid waking James, Ashley swallowed hard and walked to the table in the kitchen. Venita and Donita were cooking breakfast. Ashley sat in a chair around the kitchen table.

"Good morning everybody," Ashley said.

"Good morning Ashley. Did you sleep well," Donita said.

"Yes, I did, once I finally fell asleep," Ashley said.

Venita walked up to Ashley.

"Ashley, could I talk to you outside for a second?" Venita asked.

"Ah, sure," Ashley replied.

Ashley followed Venita out of the back door and they walked around and stood under the carport.

"Ashley, you haven't done anything to me. I just met you. I'm sorry for what I said about you last night. I was just angry and frustrated about my mother dying unexpectedly like that and shouldn't have dragged you into my mess like that. I don't apologize too often, so I hope you can forgive me," Venita said.

"Apology accepted, but James is really hurting too. I know he doesn't want hard feelings between you two," Ashley said.

"You really do care about my brother don't you? You're out here looking out for him right now," Venita said.

"I love him. He's a good man," Ashley said.

"I know he is. I've got to learn to just be happy for others when they are doing good things without thinking why I'm not doing better myself. I'll make things right between us," Venita said.

Later that morning Ashley saw James and Venita talking outside and at the end of their discussion they shared a warm embrace.

9

After going to the bank, lawyer's office and funeral home, James and Ashley finally made it to the retail superstore closest to his mother's house. As James walked down an aisle pushing a shopping cart full of drinks someone called his name.

"James. James Thomas, is that you?" a male voice said.

James turned around and two White men about the same age as James were standing in front of him.

"Daniel, is that you?" James asked.

"It's me man. I haven't seen you in forever. Hey, you remember Trevor don't you, he was on the football team too," Daniel said.

"Yeah, that's right. Sure I remember Trevor. How you doing man?" James said.

"I'm alright," Trevor said dryly.

Daniel and James caught up on old times, but Trevor said very little to James during that time. Ashley came over and joined James while placing personal care items in the shopping cart.

"Hey Ashley, these are some old friends of mine from high school," James said.

James introduced Ashley as his fiancée and soon thereafter they left the store with their purchases. James didn't know that someone else was watching their every move. Daniel and Trevor were standing outside the store watching James and Ashley leave the store's parking lot.

"Daniel, why are you always going on with these niggers we went to high school with every time you run into one of them?" Trevor asked.

"Trevor, what's your problem man. James is a good guy. He even helped me pass a couple of tests when we were in school. Did he do something to you back then?" Daniel asked.

"Look, if I didn't have to go to school with niggers and fucking Mexicans I wouldn't have. You see what happens. There he is with a White woman. That's all I'm seeing now. Mudsharks like her fucking Niggers, especially if they make good money. They would rather be a whore for a Nigger with money than be with a hard working White man who's helping to rebuild this country. Him and all his thug friends probably run trains on that White slut's pussy every night. They're probably waiting on him to bring her over right now," Trevor said as he took a drag from a cigarette.

"Look Trevor, you need to get over this shit you got in your head. Everything has changed now. We even elected a Black President. Fuck, your own sister has a half Black baby, so what's your deal?" Daniel asked.

"Yeah and I don't speak to her ass anymore because she tainted our family's blood line!" Trevor said.

"Trevor, fuck you man! You need help," Daniel said as he walked away.

Trevor took out his cell phone and called one of his friends.

"Hey Andrew, it's Trev. What's up man? Look where are you patrolling tonight. The one on the loop? Okay good. Look I was over at the Mainmart and saw this Black guy get into a black Cadillac Escalade. I think he's dirty man. I mean he looks clean cut and all, but I think he's hauling drugs or something. I thought I saw something in the back when they were loading bags into it. It has Texas plates and he has a White woman with him. Yeah I know about all that shit on the news about cops and Blacks, but we can't just close our eyes if some of these nigger thugs are pushing poison into our neighborhoods and shit. What if he gets one of your kids hooked on that shit? Alright Andrew. See you later man," Trevor said as he ended his call and smiled.

James and Ashley were on their way back to his mother's house and were about two miles away when the lights from a police cruiser lit up the road behind them.

"Is that a police car?" Ashley asked.

"Yes, it is. Maybe it's on its way to a call or something. Wait a minute, it's behind us! I'm driving at the speed limit. Okay let's see what this is about?" James said as he pulled his vehicle into a parking lot of a closed business that had lights on outside.

"James, get your driver's license and insurance card out before he walks up to your window," Ashley recommended.

"My car registration is in the center console on top. Could you get it out for me?" James asked.

Ashley did as James requested and by the time officer Andrew Walton reached the driver's side window, James had his hands resting on top of the steering wheel.

"Good evening," Officer Walton said.

"Hello officer. What's the problem?" James asked.

"I saw your vehicle drift over the center line and wanted to make sure everything was okay," Walton said.

"I don't recall that," James replied.

The officer then took his flashlight and shined the beam in Ashley's face.

"You doing okay tonight ma'am?" Walton asked.

"I'm doing fine. I'm recording this with my cell phone," Ashley informed.

The officer asked for James' driver's license and vehicle registration. After finding everything in order, another police squad car pulled up to the scene.

"Why do you need another officer? I'm confused," Ashley asked.

The other officer approached Ashley's window and then Ashley and James were asked to exit the vehicle.

"Officer, is this necessary?" James asked.

"We just need to check everything out," Walton said.

"I don't want to get out," Ashley protested.

"Ashley, go ahead. It's okay," James said as he put his hand on her arm.

Ashley and James got out of the vehicle and were both handcuffed with their hands behind their backs. While the two officers searched the vehicle and went through every bag from the store, looked under the seats and even removed the spare tire, Ashley sobbed as they sat on a curb.

"This is not right. We didn't do anything," Ashley said through tears.

Once nothing was discovered and all their belongings were placed back inside the vehicle the officers removed the handcuffs from Ashley and James. Ashley and were told they could go on about their business.

"I want both your badge numbers," James said and they were provided by both officers.

James and Ashley drove away.

"Why did they do that to us?!" Ashley screamed through tears.

"Ashley, you were just caught up in being in the car with someone who was stopped for driving while Black. If you're going to be with me, get used to it. I've been stopped plenty times for nothing, but there was always some bullshit excuse," James advised.

Ashley just looked at James in silence.

"I didn't know it was like that James. I'm sorry," Ashley said.

James and Ashley finally arrived back at their destination.

"Where were you guys? We were getting worried?" Donita said.

"We ran into a little trouble. We got stopped by a cop and he took things a little too far," James said.

"He pulled us over for no reason, well he said we drifted over the center line, but we didn't. James had his driver's license, registration and everything ready by the time the officer got to the driver's side window. Then a second cop showed up. They told us to get out of the car and they handcuffed us. We sat on the curb with our hands behind our backs while they searched the car," Ashley said.

"What?! James, you know what that was all about, the wrong color man in too nice of a whip!" Joshua said.

"Ashley, I don't want you to take this the wrong way, but a Black man in a Cadillac Escalade with a good looking White woman in the passenger seat, James, those cops went the extra mile to find something to take yo ass in for," Venita said.

"Do you think they were harder on James because of me?!" Ashley said.

"Ashley as bad as it sounds, there's probably some truth to that. It's not your fault, but some of these good ol'boys can't stand to see a Black man and White woman together," James said.

"Yeah, like your old high school friend we ran into at the store," Ashley said.

"Who, Daniel? Naw, Daniel's cool," James said.

"I'm not talking about Daniel. I'm talking about that other guy, Trevor. Yes, that was his name. He looked at me like I was trash the whole time we were standing there while you talked to them," Ashley said.

"Trevor, why does that name sound familiar? What's his last name Uncle James?" Jasmine asked.

"Trevor Daniels, I think," James said.

"I knew it! I just looked him up online. He used to be a cop, but he got kicked off the police force for racially profiling Blacks, especially Black men. It seems like there was something about his sister having a baby by a Black man that set him off," Jasmine said.

"Are you serious?" James remarked.

"The reason I remember it is because when I was in high school he harassed some of my friends for just standing and talking to each other and someone recorded the whole thing and went to one of the TV stations with it and that's how everything came out," Jamesha said.

"James, I'll bet you that racist asshole called that cop and asked him to stop us," Ashley said.

"Ashley you're probably right, but right now I want to concentrate on getting through this funeral. I didn't come down here for this other shit, but once this is over with mama, I'm filing a complaint. How much of what happened with those cops did you record?" James asked.

"I got video up until we got out of the truck and then I put my phone in my pocket before being handcuffed, but it should have picked up everything that was said," Ashley said.

Ashley played back her recording and everything was captured that was said along with video until she and James exited the vehicle.

"Ashley, you did good girl. There's no telling what they would have tried if you hadn't been recording them," Donita said.

"I've kept on top of everything that been going on. When that march was over in Dallas that night protesting police violence against African Americans and that guy started shooting policemen, I could hear the gunshots from my condo. It sent chills down my spine, so I'm sensitive to both sides of that issue," Ashley said.

"Well, I'm putting what happened tonight on the back burner. We have to approve how mama's body looks tomorrow and review everything for the funeral. That's all I want to think about right now," James said.

"James and the other adults went into the dining room and sat around the table.

"That's all I want to think about too, but I'm am worried about what will happen now that she's gone. I mean with mama gone, what about me and Jamesha? We were living here with her, but she's gone now. Can we even still stay here? I can't afford to move," Venita said.

"Look I've got the will. Why don't we all get together and read it tomorrow after we come back from the funeral home and discuss what we will do then. After what happened tonight I'm ready to go to bed and get some sleep," James said.

"Amen to that," James brother-in-law Montrel said.

After they went to bed Ashley felt compelled to tell James how she felt about the incident with the police earlier that night.

"James about what happened earlier tonight. I don't know if that guy called the police on us or not, but if he did I feel like it was because I was with you. I don't want to cause you any trouble or make your life more complicated just because you're with me," Ashley said.

"Ashley, this wasn't your fault whether Trevor called in on us or not. To guys like him, the fact that I exist at all is the problem. I don't fit the mold of what they think a Black man should be. I'm not a thug, drug dealer or in prison, so in his mind I'm out of my rightful place in this world. He thinks that his skin color makes him automatically superior to any Black man, even if that Black was President of the United States," James said.

"Well, I grew up around people that thought like him and I understand. So, you're telling me I shouldn't worry about how people feel about us being together," Ashley asked.

"Ashley, my eyes are wide open on this. I've been a Black man in America all my life. I know I have to be better, smarter and calmer than a White man in most situations in life whether it is at work or dealing with the police. If I had made a big deal about being stopped without reason or refused to get out of the car, then that would have been an escalation and gave those cops reason to arrest me. I'll handle them on the back end and still have my life, career and marriage to look forward to," James said.

"Let's get some sleep, I'm exhausted," Ashley said and gave James a kiss.

10

The next day everything was finalized for the funeral that was coming up in two days on a Saturday. When everyone was back at home, all the siblings gathered around the dining room table. Ashley decided she would go to the bedroom to give the family space. The will left behind by James' mother was simple as it divided everything equally among all her children and any proceeds left behind were to be used initially to satisfy any outstanding debt. James was named as the executor of the estate.

Everyone else in the family except Venita had their own homes in other states and did not plan to live in the family house. Since they shared equally in the estate it came to a group vote on how to work out how Venita would live in the house that they all owned equal shares in. It was decided that since Venita and Jamesha would be living there, Venita would be responsible for the property taxes, insurance and upkeep of the property that sat on a small lot on a residential street. The home was paid off from proceeds from James' father's life insurance policy when he died years before.

"Mama and I were splitting the bills! She took care of the taxes and insurance so why should I pay all of it when you guys own one fourth of everything?!" Venita asked.

"Come on Venita, you're going to be living here," Donia said.

"I think it's fair," Joshua said.

"Look Venita this house is one fourth yours, but since you will be living here it's only right that you pay the taxes, insurance and upkeep. It's not like you're paying rent. If you weren't living here we could rent the place out and split it four ways. If you, Jamesha and Keke are going to live here, that's the deal. Why should the rest of us pay for something you're getting all the use out of?" James said.

"James, are you telling me that this is a take it or leave it deal. You don't get to talk to me like that. I'm your older sister and should have been over the will, but that was mama's choice," Venita said.

"Well do you want to buy the rest of us out, Then you can do what you want," James said and the rest of the table fell silent.

Ashley could hear everything that was being said and braced for Venita's response.

"Buy you out. You know I don't have that kind of money and my credit is too bad to get a loan. You have some nerve to tell me that this is the deal. Just because you got your college degree and a big time manager's job with White folks calling you boss, you think you White. You even went and got yourself a gold digging White bitch that's ready to marry a nigga making good money! You just like the rest of those Niggas out there that once they get a little money coming in, they dump the Black women that helped them get where they were and get some trashy ass White woman willing to fuck them because they got a little money. If you were broke, she wouldn't be nowhere near your ass," Venita said.

"Venita, that's enough!" Donita said.

"Naw, Donita, it's not enough! I'm the one that was here taking care of mama and I was here when she had that heart attack. Where was James at! Probably up there fucking that White bitch! Well James, you can wallow in the dirt with that White bitch, but the White man still sees you as a nigga! Yo ass found that out when that cop pulled you over, didn't you James?!" Venita said.

James sat there fuming at what Venita was saying as she was leaning over the table pointing her finger in his face. Suddenly James sprang from his chair and lunged across the table and grabbed Venita by the throat.

"I'll kill you bitch!" James screamed as his hands were clamped around his sister's neck.

"James! Let her go man!" Joshua said as he grabbed James and tried to pull him back.

James' brother-in-law, Montrell also ran into the room and helped pulled James off Venita. James' nephews and niece, Jamesha, were looking on with their mouths open. Ashley ran from the bedroom over to James.

"James, baby, calm down!" Ashley said as she hugged him.

"I'm alright! I'm alright!" James said.

Venita was sitting in one of the dining room chair trying to catch her breath.

"He put his hands on me! I could have you locked up for assault if I called the police," Venita said.

"You ain't calling shit! I've had enough of this shit! We're supposed to be a family! Venita, I know you're the oldest, but the rest of us are not responsible for your situation. You made some bad choices in life and that's on you. Mama chose James to carry out the will and he had nothing to do with that. Bottom line is that I'm not paying part of the bills for a place that somebody else is living in, that only makes sense. You live here you pay the bills. I'm done with this shit! Mama ain't even in the ground yet and we're already at each other's throats. I'm going to bed and tomorrow we need a yes or no on what we talked about tonight," Joshua said.

Joshua was usually the quiet and reserved one in the family, but his outburst caught everybody's attention.

"James, baby. Let's go to bed," Ashley said as she led James to the bedroom.

The next day one day before the funeral and after Ashley got up she went into the kitchen.

"Venita, could I speak to you for a second outside?" Ashley asked.

"Okay," Venita said as they walked outside.

"I heard everything that happened last night and I'm not trying to get into your family's business, but what's your problem with me. You've called me a White whore, White bitch and a gold digger. I'm not any of those things. I'm your brother's fiancée. I have a good job. I'm not a whore and I met James in college when both of us didn't have a pot to piss in. Venita, I'm not afraid of you, but I want us to get along, because I'm going to be your sister-in-law and I love your brother. I'm not going to be disrespected by you all the time," Ashley said.

"Ashley, it's not that I don't like you in particular. I just don't like women like you in general. I'm not talking about those fat White trash pigs that get with a brother because some niggas will treat them like a trophy just because of their skin color. White women, especially those that could be with any man they want because they've got the education, figure and looks to be with any successful White man out there, but they know there's a lot of competition. Ya'll some ruthless bitches. Women like you know when they get older and start sagging, a White man will drop them in a hot minute for a younger, thinner and tighter model. I see it all the time with those middle aged White men walking around at the mall where I work with some twenty something year old blonde airhead on their arms. Those old men are popping blue pills to keep up with them in the bedroom. So White bitches like you, decide to switch it up and get with one of the few successful Black men out there, like my brother James, to avoid the competition. Ya'll steal our best men from us and at the same time look down your noses at the rest of the Black people around them," Venita said.

Ashley and Venita were standing nose to nose. James came into the kitchen and asked where Ashley was. Donita told him she was in the back yard talking to Venita. James looked outside and saw them talking in an animated manner.

"Venita, that is one of the most racist things I've ever heard! That's not why I'm with James! I told you we met in college when we didn't have anything!" Ashley said.

"I heard what you said, but you dropped him back then after college when he went to New York didn't you, but after he got a divorce from his Black wife and moved to Dallas with a big new job, you were all over him. James told me about what happened. You broke his heart. He was the same man back then, so what was different this time? I guess his bank account made him look a whole lot better to you now," Venita said.

Ashley stood there shocked at what Venita said to her.

"What's wrong bitch? Did the truth hurt?" Venita asked.

"You're wrong! James called me first!" Ashley said and walked away.

Venita looked on and was surprised by the last thing Ashley said to her.

Ashley walked into the kitchen and went straight to the bedroom without saying a word to James. Venita walked into the kitchen.

"Venita, what did you say to Ashley?" James asked.

"You better go talk to her," Venita said to James.

Donita looked at Venita.

"What did you say to that girl, Venita? You're my sister, but you can be a mean bitch sometimes," Donita said.

"I think I went too far this time," Venita admitted.

"Ashley what happened back there. What were you two talking about?" James asked.

"James, I love you and will support you through this funeral, but I don't know if we should get married," Ashley said.

"Ashley, what are you talking about?" James asked.

"I'm confused. I know I love you, but why didn't I go with you to New York the first time? Did I not love you enough to take a risk, but now that everything is safe it's all okay?" Ashley said.

"I don't know where this is coming from, but I've got a good idea, Venita," James said as her turned to leave.

"No James, don't ask her about anything she said to me. I can handle myself. You two need to fix whatever is broken between you, that's your sister and you are both burying your mother tomorrow," Ashley said.

"Okay. I'll give it one last shot," James said.

James went to Venita and asked her to take a ride with him. James and Venita went to a park down the street and had a long talk. Through brutal honesty and tears they worked their issues out once and for all. Venita also told James about what she said to Ashley and he told her to make it right when they got back to the house. Once they were back, Venita asked Ashley to speak with her in private in the bedroom.

"Ashley I want to apologize for what I said to you earlier. I was upset and out of line. The truth is, seeing you with James makes me feel bad about myself," Venita said.

"Venita, I don't understand," Ashley said.

"I could have been like you, but I made some bad choices. I wanted to do what I wanted and got pregnant. It wouldn't have been easy, but I could have worked my way through college, but I had to take care of my daughter. So when I see you with James, I think to myself, a man like him would look at you and me and choose you every time. I have a high school education and I'm a grandmother at thirty-eight years old. Why would a good man want someone like me over someone like you?" Venita said.

"You're thirty eight years old. How long do you think you will live?" Ashley asked.

"I don't know, seventy, if I'm lucky. That's what the bible says, three scores and ten," Venita said.

"That would mean you have thirty two years left. You have time to change how your life turns out," Ashley said.

"I don't know too many men that want to take on all the baggage I have with a daughter and grandchild to take care of," Venita said.

"What baggage? Your daughter is a grown woman. Why do you feel obligated to take care of her?" Ashley said.

"Well you know if she worked, just paying for child care would almost eat up anything she made, so I was thinking I had to carry everything until Keke went to school," Venita said.

"Where do you work?" Ashley asked.

"At the mall. I work at a Mainmart by the mall in the cosmetics and jewelry department from ten in the morning to seven thirty in the evening," Venita said.

"Does Jamsha work at all?" Ashley asked.

"No," Venita replied.

"I don't mean to get in your business, but she needs to get a job. She can work a night shift somewhere after you get home. That's her child and she needs to be able to take care of her and herself. What if something happened to you? What would she do then?" Ashley asked.

"She would probably get a job. She would have to," Venita said.

"Yep, because you wouldn't be there to carry her. Venita you have a life to live too. That's the real reason why I didn't follow James to New York. I was offered a good job in Dallas at the company I'm a manager for now. I grew up dirt poor in east Texas and we lived in an old trailer house off some back road. My folks couldn't support me if I had to come back home after college. I felt like as much as I loved James and wanted to go with him, I had to take that job in Dallas. I didn't want to have to depend on a man to take care of me. I had to make sure I could take care of myself. I want to be with James because I love him, but I don't need to be with him for financial security," Ashley said.

"You know what, you're right. I just assumed you were just one of those White women that liked Black men as a plaything, but if the going got rough, you would just flip the script and jump back to your own kind. I've seen a lot of them do it," Venita said.

"No, that's not me. I only like Black men, but I love that Black man that's your brother, James, he's something special. He makes my toes curl and…" Ashley said before Venita cut her off.

"Wait a minute, I don't need to hear all that about James, I used to change his diapers, but one day, you'll have to tell me how you, and yes I'm looking you up and down, came to only like Black men, okay," Venita said.

"Sorry about that, I almost forgot he's your brother. After all of this is over I'll tell how my addiction to chocolate men came about," Ashley said.

"Girl, you're a little crazier than I thought, but I'm feeling you. Ain't nothing like a good Black man and I'm going to find me one after all this stuff is over with mama. You know I'm going to miss her so much. I've always been with her and she been there for me. After tomorrow I can't even touch her body or look at her face anymore. I've been trying to hold it all in since I'm the oldest in the family and wanted to be strong for everybody else, but I can't anymore," Venita said as she broke down in tears.

"It's okay Venita. Let it out," Ashley said as she embraced Venita who sobbed and cried into her shoulder.

In the privacy of that small bedroom, Venita Thomas was consoled in her grief by a woman that she though represented the worst of cynical society, but turned out to be someone that would comfort her in the darkest place in her life. Afterwards Venita told her family she agreed to the arrangement for her to pays all expenses in exchange for living in the family home and apologized to everyone for her previous behavior.

The next day James and his family laid their dear mother to rest. Ashley sat on the front row with her husband to be and watched him say a sad final farewell. When they finally left Shreveport to head back to Dallas, Ashley felt closer to James than ever, because she thought she understood where he came from and saw strength in him she had not witnessed previously.

11

Once they were back in Dallas that Saturday night, Ashley decided to spend the night at James house instead of driving back to her place since it was so late. Due to the stress and cramped sleeping arrangements of the prior week, they were both exhausted. Ashley had also missed out on one of her favorite pleasures for too long and planned to rectify that situation. It was early Sunday morning and James was still asleep, but his eyes fluttered open when he felt a pleasant sensation.

"Oh Ashley, what are you doing down there baby?" James said.

Ashley did answer and then felt James hands on the back of her head and that let her know she was accomplishing her goal along with him raising his pelvis off the bed followed by a groan that came from deep inside his body.

"Oh shit!" James exclaimed.

Ashley was still silent and continued her intense attention on reviving James so she could receive some of the same pleasure she just delivered to him. After five minutes Ashley relented and straddled James with her knees on the bed on either side of his body. Ashley looked James deep into his eyes as she slowly lowered her body. When she made contact with the tip of his rock hard spear, she mouthed the words 'I love you' until her body could not descend any longer. Ashley then threw her head back and began to slam her body down onto James in a rapid fashion. James occupied his hands by filling them with Ashley firm breasts with their excited nipples wedged between his fingers. Ashley began to moan as she suddenly started to jerk her hips forward and shudder.

"Oh God! I love you James," Ashley said and fell onto his chest.

"Ashley, we need to set a date. I want to wake up like this every morning," James said.

"Me too, but don't count on me being your alarm clock like this every day. This was a special treat, you know like breaking a diet with your favorite desserts all at once, but I'm ready to become Mrs. Ashley Riley-Thomas," Ashley said.

"Riley-Thomas, so you want to do the hyphenated name thing?" James questioned.

"Well yes, I thought about it. Is that a problem?" Ashley said.

"I don't think so. I'm just used to wives taking their husbands' last name," James said.

"James relax. I'll be happy to be Mrs. Ashley Thomas. I can already tell your ego would be conflicted by taking my last name. James, you're such a cave man, but you're my cave man and I love you," Ashley said.

"I prefer to think of myself as traditional, not a cave man, thank you very much, woman," James said with a laugh.

"James, I was proud of you for the way you handled things with your family. It was very responsible of you to take out a life insurance policy on your mother. I guess you could see something like what happened coming. I didn't know how difficult things would be between you and Venita, except for you choking her of course, but you handled it well and seemed to finally have worked things out," Ashley said.

"Yeah, that was very rough. I just lost it. I didn't expect Venita to react the way she did and for her to constantly attack you for no reason just made it worse. I know she's my older sister, but that wasn't about her situation. Everything that week should have been about mama and making sure she was put away in a way that would have made her proud. The rest of it was Venita being all in her feelings, but she seemed to be doing better when we left. By the way you never shared what you and Venita talked about, but she seemed to have a different opinion of you when we left, so what happened between you two?" James asked.

"After you and Venita got back that day after you talked, we went into the bedroom and just talked like grown women. Venita is hurt and her self-esteem was in the gutter. I can see how she felt like a failure in life, because she's the oldest and from her point of view all of her younger siblings passed her by. You are her younger brother and have an important and high paying manager's job with a huge company. Joshua basically owns his own business and works for himself with his trucking business. Donita has a husband, children and her own home. All of you moved away and there she was stuck at home with her young daughter and then when her daughter followed in her footsteps and got pregnant young, Venita felt responsible for setting a bad example. She felt like she not worthy of being loved by a man, like she's damaged goods. I told her that was crazy and that she had a lot to live for and that she is not responsible for taking care of her grown daughter. I also told Venita that she could find a man that would love her. A man like you," Ashley said.

"Thank you for telling my sister something she wouldn't take coming from me, but she won't find another man like me! There aren't any other men like me out there. You got the last one," James said.

"Oh my God.! You're ego is so big that I can hardly fit in the same room with you," Ashley said as she playfully hit James with a pillow.

"Hey, I'm calling the police department in Shreveport tomorrow and filing a formal complaint against that officer and bringing up Trevor's name so they can look into it," James said.

"Okay, I'm behind you one hundred percent, because I think something stinks about the way that happened," Ashley said.

"I'm hitting the shower and you need to decide on a wedding date and all the other details women worry about for a wedding," James said.

"Aren't you going to help?" Ashley asked.

"Sure, I'll be standing up front waiting on you when you walk down that aisle," James said.

"James please!" Ashley said as he walked into the bathroom.

Ashley went back to work and it took her a week to dig through her emails and catch up on what was going one since she had left a week prior.

"So how was everything and how is James doing?" Janeka asked Ashley.

"James is holding up pretty good and it was a lovely and sad funeral since his mother died so suddenly," Ashley said.

"How was it meeting his family?" Janeka asked.

"It was good for the most part, except for his sister Venita," Ashley asked

"What was the problem with his sister?" Janeka asked.

"She just hated my ass from the very beginning. She called me a White whore, White bitch and a gold digger. It got very intense," Ashley said.

"What, but she didn't even know you," Janeka said.

"I know, but it was what I represented. Venita had this thing about how some White women cherry pick what she sees as the best Black men and take them away from the Black women out there having a hard time finding a good Black man. She thought some White women like me that could have an eligible White man do it to avoid competing with other White women for a desirable White guy. She thinks we don't want to worry about getting dumped for a younger woman as we get older," Ashley said.

"Well Ashley, to be honest with you. I've thought about that myself," Janeka said.

"What, are you serious?!" Ashley responded in surprise.

"Not about you, but I think some White women think a Black man will be more likely to stick with them for the long run. I see successful White guys refreshing their wives all the time as they get older," Janeka said.

"Refreshing their wives, holy shit!" Ashley said.

"Why do you think those White women are getting face lifts, filler injected into their faces and breast implants all the time if they can afford it?

They're trying to compete with little young sluts hanging around every corner willing to knock them out of the way if their husbands are willing to give them a try," Janeka said.

"Yes, but don't Black men get divorced and remarried to younger women too?" Ashley asked.

"Yeah, some of them do, but there're not enough Black men well off enough to afford the financial hit of a divorce settlement and still be able to live a comparable lifestyle that the other woman would be satisfied with afterwards. A lot of these younger Black women out there know the married man they're a side chick for is not leaving his wife for them, so they settle for side-bitch benefits, you know getting their hair style paid for or getting a little financial help here and there. If a younger White chick is giving up that nookie to an older married White man on a consistent basis, she's going to ask where that relationship is going and if he not giving her the right answers, another target is around the corner. We don't have as many desirable Black men to choose from. Take James for example, I can count on one hand how many Black men I personally know that have the type of position and earning power he does. I'm not talking about athletes, politicians or entertainers, but real world people. Finding a Black man like James, that wants to get married, you don't know how lucky you are," Janeka said.

"I don't know Janeka. I haven't noticed any other women coming at James when I'm around," Ashley said.

"They aren't going to be that bold, but with all this social media stuff going on with apps that let people looking for hookups find each other under the radar you would never know, it's a whole new world. If James wanted to he could have a full schedule of thots on rotation sliding into his DM, but that rock he put on your finger is a good sign that he doesn't think that way and has found what he's looking for. Anyway, were you able to make peace with his sister?" Janeka asked.

"Yes, we came to an understanding. She's just frustrated and under financial pressure. She feels like as the oldest in the family, she should be doing better financially than her younger siblings. I think her pride is hurt and Venita doesn't think she gets the respect she deserves," Ashley said.

"I can relate to that, because sometimes the oldest children in many Black families feel like they got shortchanged. Some dropped out of school to help support the family or couldn't go straight to college, because they helped with their younger brothers and sisters. I've seen that a lot. What does she do for a living?" Janeka asked.

"She works in retail at a Mainmart in Shreveport in the cosmetics and jewelry department. Janeka said she has worked there for several years. I hate to ask, but we have a store in Shreveport. Would you entertain giving someone like Janeka a chance in your jewelry sales operation there?" Ashley said.

"That would be interesting. Those places just pay by the hour. If she was good enough and worked at a higher end jewelry department, she could make salary and commission. That makes a difference. I don't know her, her capabilities or anything about her, but why don't you pass her resume along to me. I don't know if the jewelry manager needs anyone, but I might be able to put in a word, but I would need to see how she looks on paper first," Janeka.

"I think Venita has potential, but she might need some polishing to fit in with our target market," Ashley said.

"I understand that, but we have a good two week training program. Everything is scripted until someone learns to ropes and can put the sales presentation in their own words. Each product line of watches, for example, has a video history and overview. It could take some work on her part, but if she's intelligent enough to learn the products, materials and sales pitches, it could work," Janeka said.

"I'm surprised you're willing to stick your neck out for this woman you don't even know?" Ashley asked.

"There's this thought in the Black community that we don't lend a helping hand to each other. I'm not like that. If I can't at least give another Black person a shot, and that's all it is, then why was I busting my ass to get into this position, just so I could say look at me, I made it, but the hell with the rest of you. Doing something like this is no risk for me. We hire people every day that don't work out. If something develops and she gets hired, success or failure is on her," Janeka said.

"Okay, I'll talk to Venita and see what she thinks," Ashley said.

"Let me know. I'll see you later," Janeka said as she got up to leave.

"Thank you Janeka," Ashley said.

"Why do you want to help her after the way she treated you?" Janeka asked,

"Venita was so sad and saw no hope for the future. Everyone deserves hope," Ashley said.

12

Ashley settled on a wedding date in June, but where to have the ceremony was an open question since Ashley lived in Dallas, her parents lived in Galveston and she grew up in Lufkin. Lufkin won out since most of the friends Ashley grew up with were from there and she wanted everyone to see she wasn't trashy Ashley any longer. Ashley wanted her childhood friend, Latrisha Johnson, to be her maid of honor. James was in full agreement with Ashley's wedding plans, but he just wished his mother was still alive to see him as a complete man again.

One month after filing a complaint with the Shreveport police department James got a response. The officer that stopped James when he was driving from Mainmart admitted that he had no valid reason to pull the vehicle over. When asked if someone encouraged him to stop James, the officer cracked and admitted that Trevor tipped him off about James. Officer Walton was suspended without pay and Trevor was charged with filing a false report. James felt a small sense of victory in what had seemingly been a war on the dignity of Black men by those sworn to protect them.

James came back home from his routine two mile run on a Saturday and found Ashley on her phone while she was typing on her laptop computer. James went to the bathroom and took a shower.

"Who were you on the phone with?" James asked.

"Venita," Ashley asked.

"Venita? My sister Venita?" James said.

"Yes, your sister Venita," Ashley replied.

"Is something wrong?" James asked.

"No, I was just helping her with something," Ashley replied.

"Come on Ashley, what's going on?" James asked.

"If you must know, I'm helping Venita with her resume', she's applying for a sales position in the jewelry department of our store in Shreveport," Ashley said.

"Excuse me! Venita is applying for a position with your company. You guys are pretty high end. Venita works in a big box discount store. How is that going to work?" James remarked.

"James you need to have a little more faith in your big sister. If she presents herself properly, those people dealing with her won't have a clue about her background. Janeka is pulling a few strings to help her get in. I've coached her on how she should dress and talk. This could be big for her?" Ashley said.

"Okay. We'll see what happens," James said.

Ashley could hear the doubt in James voice in regard to his sister's prospects for success in her new venture. Ashley continued to work on Venita's resume and when it was complete she emailed it to Venita who would print it out at a nearby office supply store. Venita had an interview and later secured the open position, the rest was up to her. As for Ashley, she entered a period of time where she concentrated on work and her wedding.

Ashley made several visits back to her home town to plan for her wedding. The church that would host the wedding ceremony was the largest African American Baptist Church in town and was the home church of her friend Latrisha. The pastor knew Ashley from her attending service with Latrisha and her family when she was younger. Janeka was also assisting with planning the wedding and would be a bridesmaid along with one other friend of Ashley's and to Venita's surprise, Ashley asked her to be a bridesmaid also.

The week of the ceremony the wedding party assembled in Lufkin, Texas to run through rehearsals and final fittings.

"Latrisha! It's so good to see you girl!" Ashley said after she pulled into the driveway of her old friend's childhood home.

Latrisha was standing at the driver's side window of Ashley's car before walking around and getting into the passenger side seat.

"Ashley, it's been a long time girl," Latrisha said as they hugged over the console in the car between the front seats.

"With you living all the way out there in LA, we talk on the phone, but I miss our face to face time," Ashley said.

Latrisha was an impressive woman who continued her education beyond undergraduate and earned a PHD in mathematics and was employed as a research analyst for a polling company. Latrisha was considered a super independent Black woman. James had his issues with Latrisha, because he felt she helped persuade Ashley not to go to New York with him after they left college.

"So here we are. After all those years, you and James are getting married. Is he still pissed off at me?" Latrisha asked.

"You're not his favorite person. He thinks you pushed your Black superwoman ideas on me. You know, I don't need a man, was your favorite comeback," Ashley said.

"Yeah I know, I know, and I told you that you shouldn't follow him and give up your independence. Look, I was so crazy and mixed up back then. After college I still felt like I didn't need a man, but later I found out I needed a good woman instead," Latrisha said.

"What? What are you talking about?" Ashley asked.

"I met this woman at a party and that's when I finally admitted to myself that I was attracted to women. I'm a lesbian and living an openly gay lifestyle. I'm engaged!" Latrisha said as she displayed an engagement ring on her finger.

"What, to a woman?!" Ashley asked while still stunned.

"Yes, to a woman, her name is Tanisha and she came here with me to meet my folks," Latrisha said.

"I can't believe you never told me," Ashley said.

"I didn't know how just throw it in during a phone call. You know, oh, by the way, I'm fucking women now. You know, awkward," Latrisha said.

"Congratulations, but shit, I thought taking James to meet my parents was tough. Your dad is a deacon in a Baptist church. How did he react?" Ashley asked.

"He was not happy. That went against everything he believed in. I hate to admit it, but the Black church is one of the least supportive of the gay lifestyle, but he came around because he loves me. He stepped down from being a deacon at the church. Dad felt it would be hypocritical to stay on. That hurt me the most, for him, but it showed how much he cared about me," Latricia said.

"Did he blame you?" Ashley asked.

"No, Dad said it opened his eyes. He said it's not as easy to condemn someone for their lifestyle when it's someone you love," Latrisha said.

"I guess that kind of what happened with my father and Black men. He didn't like it or understand it, but after I explained things he came around. You know we started out as roommates in college, I never suspected you were gay back then," Ashley said.

"Back then I was still fucking guys, so I hadn't figured it out yet either," Latrisha said.

"I feel like I can ask you anything since we've known each other so long, but were you in a relationship with someone, you know, a man, when you met Tanisha?" Ashley asked.

"Yes his name was Xavier. We had been together for six months. After I figured out what was going on with me, I broke it off with him. He was so hurt and confused, but I didn't cheat on him, I couldn't do that," Latrisha said.

"Wow, I'm surprised, but happy for you," Ashley said.

"Well enough about me. Are you excited?" Latrisha asked. "

"Yes, I'm very excited. I'm ready to become James' wife and hopefully start a family soon. Do you ever feel like you've lived two different lives, I mean the life we lived down here and the life you're living now?"Ashley asked.

"Definitely, I feel like I was so unexposed to the rest of the world while I was here. All I really saw was that I had a certain place in the world before I left here and it was very limited, but now I know I can go as far as my abilities will take me. My skin color, gender or my sexual orientation doesn't matter. Every time I come back here it's like going back to your elementary school and everything looks so much smaller than I remember," Latrisha said.

"That's exactly how I feel. I was less than dirt to the other White kids around here when I was growing up. I was trashy Ashley, the poor trailer trash girl. Do you remember when we went out with those two football players when we were in the eleventh grade?" Ashley asked

"Derrick Johnson and Franklin Jones, I remember that. They took us to a house party and later on over to Derrick's older brother's house while he was out of town. Derrick got me naked that night, but the only thing he got inside me was his finger," Latrisha said.

"What?! You told me you did it with him that night. I did it with Franklin, that was my first time," Ashley said.

"I didn't want to seem like a pussy, so I lied. I gave him some the next time we went out though," Latrisha said.

"I guess I better get going and let you get back inside before your fiancée thinks we have something going on," Ashley said.

"You don't have to worry about that. Tanisha knows you're not my type. You're too skinny and White. I like my women thick and dark, the same way you like your men," Latricia said.

"Too skinny and White, you know what, Latrisha, you can still be an asshole after all these years," Ashley said.

"Yes, but I'm your asshole, and your maid of honor. I'll see at the wedding rehearsal tomorrow night and you can meet Tanisha then. Bye, love you Ashley," Latricia said as she walked back to the house.

Ashley appreciated that Latrisha let her know about what was going on before the wedding, so she would not have any last minute surprises. Ashley left and needed to make a stop at a store to pick up a few items before heading to the hotel where James and her parents were staying.

13

Ashley stopped by the local Mainmart to pick up some cleaning supplies to sanitize the hotel rooms everyone was staying in. After Ashley checked out and was about to exit the store someone called out to her.

"Ashley Riley, is that you?" a woman said.

Ashley turned around and a woman about her age with red hair was standing in front of her.

"I'll bet you don't remember me do you?" the woman said.

Ashley looked closely at the woman and although she seemed vaguely familiar, she could not recall who she was.

"It's me, Rebecca Strickland, well Rebecca Norman now, we went to school together," Rebecca said.

"Oh yeah, hi Rebecca. I remember you now. How are you doing?" Ashley said as they moved to the side out of the path of people entering and leaving the store.

"I'm doing okay, but we don't have the business like we did back then, so I'm selling real estate. I saw your marriage announcement in the newspaper and the picture of you and your fiancée. Is he from here?" Rebecca asked.

"No, he's from Louisiana," Ashley replied.

"You know I married Evan Norman. You remember him. He was the quarterback on the football team," Rebecca said.

"Oh yeah, I remember Evan," Ashley said.

Ashley declined to inform Rebecca that her husband was constantly trying to get her to have sex with him behind her back when they were in high school.

"I know we didn't really talk much in school, but I remember when you used to live in that old trailer house..." Rebecca said before Ashley cut her off.

"Alright Rebecca, cut it out. We were never friends in school, okay. You know that and I know that. You thought you were better than I was and called me trashy Ashley. That was a long time ago and I don't live in that trailer anymore. I live in a high rise condo overlooking downtown Dallas," Ashley said.

"Why are you acting so offended? I was just talking about old times since you were back in town after all these years to get married to your fiancée. I noticed that he's a Black man. You used to hang around the Black kids in school. Just saying," Rebecca said.

"What's that supposed to mean?" Ashley asked while trying to control her temper.

"You know Ashley, it's not what someone has that makes them a certain way, but their attitude and who they associate with. I just think it's strange that you couldn't find a respectable White man to marry you. You're just a slutty mudshark," Rebecca said.

"Rebecca, we aren't in school anymore. I'm not trying to be in your circle of cool girls and you don't get to decide who has class or not. My future husband is a great man. He has a good job, a college education and we love each other," Ashley said.

"Well trash is as trash does. No self respecting White woman would open her legs for a nigger to have his way with her. You're still trashy Ashley," Rebecca said.

"Rebecca, what is your problem? I haven't seen you in years. Is it because you're not on top anymore? You were a big fish in a small pond and that was it. Rebecca, you could keep your legs open all day long and my fiancée wouldn't fuck you with somebody else's dick, but what you really need to open is that small mind of yours. Have a good day, bitch! By the way your husband was trying to get me to fuck him behind your back all the time when we were in high school. He wasn't my type," Ashley said as she left the store.

Rebecca just stood there with her mouth hanging open. Ashley felt energized because this was the first time in her life that she had to chance to stand up to her old bully from the past on her own. Ashley went back to the hotel and later James, Ashley and her parents all went out to dinner.

"I ran into Rebecca Strickland when I went to the store earlier. She's married now, to the guy that used to be the quarterback for our high school football team, Evan Norman," Ashley said.

"Who's Rebecca?" James asked.

"Rebecca, I guess you could say was the leader of the cool girls in school. She considered me to be poor White trash and not worthy enough to be friends with her and her clique. She was a bitch then and is still one now," Ashley said.

"What, did she say something to you?" Gregory asked.

"Yes! At first she acting all nice and then she started in on me about how getting married to a Black man still makes me White trash. She called me a mudshark," Ashley said.

"Mudshark, what's a mudshark?" Katherine asked.

"It's an ugly word used for White woman that date Black men. Some people think White women that date Black guys have a self esteem problem or are trying to rebel against their parents or something. It's just another stupid and racist thing for someone to call somebody else, like I'm contaminated or something," Ashley eplained.

"That's awful. Honey, you don't feel that way do you?" Katherine asked.

141

"Of course not, it's just a nasty thing to say. Why can't people just accept what other people want and keep their opinions to themselves?" Ashley said.

"Did you say something back to her?" Edward asked.

"I basically told her to go fuck herself," Ashley said.

"Well, that's what you should have told her. Stupid bitch!" Katherine said.

"Mom! I've never heard you curse before," Ashley said.

"Well, she's just angry about how everything fell apart for them once they lost that poultry business after it was shut down. She's just like everybody else now and can't look down on other people, she just hasn't figured it out yet," Edward said.

"Look Ashley, most people don't care what other people do or who they do it with, but there are still a lot of people out there that still hold on to ideas that people of different races shouldn't marry each other. We know it's stupid, but it makes some people like Trevor, back in Louisiana, mad as hell. As much as I hate to say it, those attitudes aren't going away anytime soon. We are going to be married and some people are going to think the same thing about you as Rebecca, are you ready for that?" James said.

"I can take it. Those kind of people don't bother me and don't affect my life," Ashley said.

"What if it was your boss and he was holding you back because of how he felt about you being married to me?" James said.

"How would I even know something like that was going on? I'm already dealing with those thoughts in the back of my mind because I'm a woman. All I can do is live my life with the man I love and deal with whatever else comes my way," Ashley said with a sigh.

"You know honey, James is right. I have some guys I work with that hate the thought of their daughters dating Black men. They think White men have been passed over, because those in power wanted Black, Hispanics and women to get ahead at their expense. With the politics going on today, they feel like they can say out loud what they used to talk about just among themselves. One guy told me when he saw a White woman with a Black man, it was like they had taken the last thing a White man had to hold on to. I told him my daughter was getting married to a Black man that was a good, decent and hard working American. He looked at me like I had a contagious disease and hadn't said a word to me since. Fuck him," Edward said as he took a sip of coffee.

"Dad!" Ashley said.

"No, I'm serious. He's a dinosaur with a rebel flag decal on his pickup truck. The Civil War is over, but some people are still fighting it. James, let me say this to you. You've shown me that you love Ashley and want the best for her. That's all I could ask of any man that will be my son in law," Edward said.

"Mr. Riley, I appreciate that and I will take care of your daughter," James said.

"Mr. Riley? It will be dad in a few days," Edward said.

Late that night while they were in bed, James asked Ashley a question she didn't expect to come from him.

"Ashley, do you feel like you're hurting yourself by marrying me?" James asked.

"Hurting myself, James, what are you talking about?" Ashley asked.

"I mean the looks, your father's initial objections and just outright hate from some people. Some people think you must have something wrong with you to marry a Black man. Will you wake up one day, look at me and decide you made a mistake and walk away?" James asked.

"James, I'm not marrying a Black man, I'm marrying you and you just happen to be Black. I could ask you the same questions. I been told that maybe I'm taking the easy way out, by not competing with all the ruthless White women for a desirable White man or that I taking one of the few desirable Black men from Black women, your own sister said that. Will you wake up one day and look over at me and ask, what are you doing with that skinny White woman when you could have your pick of beautiful Black women out there and skip the extra drama of being with me? I see how they look at you when we're together. They're thinking that you don't know what you're missing by being with me when they could put all that ass they have on you," Ashley said.

"Okay, you are so crazy. I love your skinny ass," James said as he rolled over on top of Ashley.

"You do, then show me," Ashley said.

James started kissing Ashley and rubbed his hand between her thighs as she squirmed. James lifted her nightgown and freed himself from his underwear. Ashley welcomed James into her embrace. Ashley looked James in his eyes.

"Don't fuck me too hard baby. You need to save some for our honeymoon," Ashley said with a smile.

Ashley's words seemed to do something to James as he drove into her with a fresh vigor. After thirty minutes they both reveled in release.

"Damn baby, you do love my skinny ass don't you," Ashley said.

"Yes I do and you will keep getting that forever," James said.

Three days later James and Ashley were married with their family and friends present. Ashley was a radiant bride dressed in an all white gown with a flowing train. The wedding was a clash of cultures with Blacks and Whites of all generations in attendance. During the wedding reception a popular line dance anthem blasted from the speakers of the DJ's sound system. Ashley rushed to the dance floor with Janeka, Latrisha and Venita alongside her.

"Ashley, do you know how to wobble?" Venita asked.

"Just watch me," Ashley said.

Ashley rotated her hips to the beat of the song and was in perfect step with all the other women on the dance floor.

"What in the world are they doing?" Edward asked.

"I don't know, but it looks like fun," Katherine said as she walked onto the dance floor alongside Ashley.

"Come on mama, do it like this!" Ashley instructed as Katherine followed along.

"Oh my lord," Edward said as he watched.

"Looks like you're going to have to learn how to dance now," James said to Edward with a laugh.

Two days later, Ashley woke up and looked out of her window and the Pacific Ocean waters were rolling onto the beach in front of their hotel in Honolulu, Hawaii.

"James, come look at this view," Ashley said as she stood in front of the glass patio door in her mid-thigh length nightgown.

James walked up behind her.

"The best view I saw was you standing here while I was still in bed. Do you remember when we first made love after I moved to Dallas?" James asked.

"Yes. It was at my condo while I was looking out of the patio door. James, what are you doing? What if someone sees us?" Ashley said as James sunk to his knees behind her while she still looked out of the window.

"They can't see me behind you," James said as he raised the back of Ashley's nightgown with his head going underneath.

Ashley slightly widened her stance as she looked out at the blue water.

"Ahh," Ashley said as James tongue lashed between her thighs.

Ashley pushed her buttocks backwards slightly to allow James better access to his target. James' tongue began to play a melody on Ashley's private area and she was breathing heavenly. James stood behind Ashley and she stood on the tip of her toes. As James stood he also entered the object of his desire. Ashley continued to look forward and to anyone that may have been looking from the beach below all they saw was a woman looking out of a glass balcony door.

"Ah, yes James. Fuck me baby," Ashley said.

"Do you love me baby?" James asked.

"Yes. I love you James," Ashley answered.

"Do you love my Black dick in your White pussy?" James asked as he pumped away.

"Yes baby, I love your Black dick in my White pussy," Ashley replied.

Ashley then felt a sensation she hadn't experienced since that first night in her condo as James wet finger that was wet from their combined juices snaked it way into her rear passage as he still pumped into her.

"Oh my God baby. You're sliding your finger into my ass. Shit!" Ashley said.

"Yes, I am baby," James said as he increased his lovemaking rhythm.

"Oh yes baby. Fuck me harder," Ashley encouraged.

Suddenly James withdrew and repositioned himself.

"Do you want it back there baby?" James asked.

"Yes, baby. I want it back there," Ashley replied.

"Then come get it," James said.

Ashley was on fire sexually. Ashley slowly and forcefully pushed her hips backwards toward James until she felt entry.

"Oh fuck!" Ashley exclaimed.

"Fuck me Ashley," James requested.

Ashley began to move her hips back and forth while James remained stationary.

"Goddamn James. You're fucking my ass baby," Ashley said.

"No, baby, you're fucking your own ass. I'm just your instrument. Now give it to me faster," James said.

"Oh! Oh!" Ashley said as she slammed her ass back in James body.

Suddenly Ashley tensed and shuddered. James pulled Ashley away from the door and carried her to the bed when her place her with her knees on the floor while her face rested on her arms on the bed. James grasped Ashley by her waist and drove into her rapidly.

"Ungh! Ungh!" James groaned as he felt a primal release and collapse onto Ashley's back.

Ashley reached her hand back and stroked James on his neck. James and Ashley both crawled onto the bed and lay there panting.

"Damn James. I didn't know I could come from being fucked in the ass, but I did. I would never let any other man do that to me but you.

That's only the second time you've done that to me. Why then and why now?" Ashley asked.

"When we did that the first time, it was the first time I've ever did that. I wanted to do something with you that I have done with no one else and figured if you let me do that it showed me how much you trusted me. This time I did it to show you how much I love you. Ashley, I want you in every way I can have you. I love you that much," James said.

"Then you better clean up and get that thing up again. I like that other way too, but I want you to fuck me until I go to sleep with you inside me. That's how much I love you," Ashley said.

James hurried to the bathroom and they never made it out of the hotel room that day with room service bringing meals whenever they got hungry.

"Look at these people over here. They are a mixture of races. I can see all kind of features in their faces of people from all over the world. It's amazing," Ashley said as they walked along the beach.

"Yeah, I was reading that Hawaii has the most multiracial population in the United States, but there are racial problems here too," James said.

"Really, but everyone seems so nice," Ashley said.

"It's really more like what happened to the American Indians. Your people overthrew the kingdom and took the islands away from the native Hawaiians. There are a lot of native Hawaiians around and they are still pissed about it. So watch your ass, White woman," James said.

"My people, White woman, what the hell are you talking about?" Ashley said.

"I'm just saying. I could always say I don't know you if the shit hits the fan," James said with a laugh.

"You wouldn't do that. You know you love my skinny ass," Ashley said as she kissed James on the cheek.

"You're right," James said with a smile.

14

James and Ashley arrived back home and began their life together as a married couple. Ashley moved in with James and sold her condo because they determined if they were going to have children it made more sense to live in the larger house. Three months after they were married, Ashley informed James she was pregnant. Ashley was thrilled, James was happy, but Ashley's mother was overjoyed.

"Ashley, you finally did it. I hope it's a little girl then I can dress her up and everything, but if it's a boy, I can spoil him rotten too," Katherine said.

"Mama, it will still be a while before you're a grandmother," Ashley said.

"Well, it can't be soon enough for me," Katherine said.

James and Ashley worked, lived and prepared to become new parents. On a sunny Wednesday morning in June before James went to work, Ashley told him that her water broke. James went into full preparing to have a baby mode and grabbed Ashley's bag that was already packed, before leading her to the SUV for the ride to the hospital. Twenty two hours after arriving at the hospital, James and Ashley were the new parents of a baby boy they named Ashton James Thomas. Ashley's parents had driven to Dallas and were in the delivery room when their first grandchild was born.

"James, look at him. He's so beautiful. He has your eyes, my nose and his skin color is a mix of the both of us," Ashley said.

"Yes he is. This is our son," James said.

James and Ashley both took family leave which allowed them to bond with their son. Ashley decided to breastfeed Ashton due to the health benefits for her baby and herself. Ashley worked hard to get her body back in shape and by the time she went back to work she was pleased with the results.

"Welcome back mama!" Janeka said as she went into Ashley's office.

"It's good to be back, but I miss my little man," Ashley said.

"James will be fine," Janeka said.

"You know I'm not talking about James," Ashley said as she showed her phone to Janeka with an image of Ashton as the lock screen.

"He's such a cutie. Listen, I'll let you get to work because you have a lot to catch up on," Janeka said.

It took Ashley over two weeks to get her feet back under her at work, but she also found her job to be less stressful because her perspective on life had changed since she became a mother. Her son and family became her number one priority with career goals being placed in their proper role.

As Aston grew his true physical characteristics began to emerge. With a skin tone that resembled a perfect tan combined with a thick, curly head of hair that was somewhere between brunette and blonde, Aston was a balanced combination of his parents physical characteristics. In addition to being a beautiful baby, Ashton was the pride of Ashley's parent's eyes. Edward couldn't wait until his grandson got older so he could teach him how to fish and had already bought a child sized fishing tackle set for him.

Two years after Ashton's birth Ashley felt she was top of the world with the perfect child, marriage and career. Once again Ashley was rewarded with the honor of going on her company's annual recognition trip for her team's performance. The trip that year was to Palm Beach, Florida with luxury accommodations, celebrity treatment and a variety of activities. Ashley's parents kept Ashton while she and James were out of town.

Ashley and James flew to Florida and the pampering began at the airport where they were greeting by someone holding a sign with their names on it. After being driven to a historic luxury hotel situated next to the Atlantic Ocean, Ashley and James exited a chauffeur driven limousine and felt like royalty. As they walked into the storied property that catered to wealthy guests, celebrities and royalty, Ashley and James were amazed at the opulence surrounding them.

"So this is how the one percent lives?" James said.

"You know, I understand how blessed we are to have our life, our son and careers, but this is just amazing. I watched one of those travel shows and this place will provide almost anything their guests want. One guest wanted a piano in his room and they got it for him. Another one wanted a meal made out of that fish, you know, if it's not prepared just right the poison can kill you, and they flew a chef in that could prepare it for her," Ashley said.

"Wow," James said.

Ashley and James walked into a reception hall set up for those coming on the trip to gather and mingle.

"Hi James, how you doing," a woman's voice said from behind him.

James recognized the voice immediately, but it couldn't belong to who he thought it was. James turned around with a glass of wine in his hands.

"Venita! What are you doing here?" James asked almost in shock as he looked into the face of his oldest sister.

"I was number one in sales in our district last year. I won this trip," Venita informed.

James turned to Ashley.

"Did you know about this?" James asked.

"Yes I did, and we wanted to surprise you," Ashley said with a mischievous smile.

"I don't know what to say," James said.

"How about congratulations to your sister?" Ashley said.

"Congratulations, of course. Venita, you look great. Did you lose some weight?" James asked.

"James, you don't ask a woman something like that in public," Ashley said.

"Oh, sorry," James said.

A handsome Black man about twenty-nine years old walked up alongside Venita and gave her a glass of wine.

"Dashon, this is my brother James and his wife Ashley. Ashley helped me get this job," Venita said.

"It's nice to meet you. Venita talks about you two all the time," Dashon said.

"It's nice to meet you too. So, you're my sister's boyfriend?" James asked.

"I'm her man and she's my boo," Dashon said as he planted a kiss on Venita's cheek.

"Dashon came into the store looking for a new watch and I helped him out. Later on he came back and asked me out," Venita said.

"I guess you saw more than just a watch that you liked in the jewelry department, didn't you Dashon?" Ashley said.

"I liked the watch and already knew I wanted it before I walked in, but I acted like I didn't know anything about it so I could spend more time with Venita," Dashon said.

"That's so sweet. Do your thing girl," Ashley said as Venita laughed.

"Hey guys. I'm worn out and ready to get some sleep. It's nice to meet you Dashon, and Venita, congratulations again. I'm proud of you and mama would be so proud if she could see you now," James said as he kissed his sister on her cheek.

"James, you don't know how much it means to me to hear you say that. Thank you," Venita said as she embraced her younger brother.

"Venita, are you crying?" James asked.

"I just got a little emotional thinking about mama. I'll see you guys later," Veinita replied.

James and Ashley walked away toward the elevators and went to their tenth story room that overlooked the beach below.

"James, you should have seen the look on your face when you first saw Venita," Ashley said as they sat in their room looking out toward the Atlantic Ocean in the darkness.

"I was shocked. Venita was the last person I expected to see here. I guess I never thought about how she was doing in her job. Do you remember when I asked you what you were doing that night when you told me you were helping her with her resume'?" James said.

"Yeah, I remember that. What about it?" Ashley said.

"It just makes me wonder about something. How was it that you saw something in my own sister that I couldn't see? I never thought Venita could achieve something like this," James said.

"Sometimes those nearest to us are so close that they can't see us like a stranger can, with fresh eyes. In your mind Venita was your older sister who had made mistakes in her life and was full of regret and bitterness. I saw someone hungry for a second chance to change her destiny. Venita has busted her ass at work and it paid off. Janeka will give her a trophy tomorrow night and a one thousand dollar bonus check," Ashley said.

"That's why I love you so much. Ashley, Venita wasn't very nice to you when you first met her, but you went the extra mile and changed my sister's life. Thank you," James said.

"Everybody deserves a chance to be the best they can be in life. Nobody thought I would amount to anything either. That bitch, Rebecca, told me in high school that she heard the strip clubs were hiring White trash so I should go apply. That's what

I mean by those around you can't see past their image of who they think you are," Ashley said.

"You're not White trash, but you can strip for me anytime. You're even more beautiful now that you're my wife and the mother of my son," James said.

James took out his phone a selected a song with a rhythmic bass beat.

"So you want me to do a striptease dance right here in this hotel room?" Ashley asked.

"Why not? We're here all alone with the ocean right outside our window," James said.

"What if someone sees us?" Ashley asked.

"It's dark outside. There's nobody out there on the beach," James said.

Ashley looked around. James took his money clip out of his pocket and pulled out a huge stack of twenty dollar bills.

"What are you doing carrying all that cash on you?" Ashley asked.

"I like to roll with at least a thousand on me. You never know when you might need some cash," James said as he folded a twenty in half and waved it at Ashley.

"Really! That money is half mine already since we have a joint bank account. I don't even know how to do a stripper dance," Ashley said.

"That's okay. I'll reward effort," James said.

Ashley turned her back to James and began to sway her hips from side to side to the beat of the music. James sat in the chair watching every move his wife made as she unzipped the back of her dress and slowly allowed it to drop to the floor. James took his folded twenty and slipped it under the elastic waistband of Ashley's panties. Ashley then reached her hands around her back and removed her bra and turned to face James. James tried to touch Ashley, but she brushed his hands away.

"You know the rules, No touching," Ashley said.

"How much for a lap dance?" James asked.

"Two hundred," Ashley replied.

"Two hundred! Damn!" James said as he peeled off ten twenty dollar bills.

"I'm worth it," Ashley said.

Ashley then placed her arms on each side of James head with her hands gripping the back of the Queen Ann style chair. Ashley then moved her body down and James face came within a half inch of her breasts as they passed by. Turning around with her back facing James again, Ashley held her body weight up by gripping the arms of the chair. With her panties still on Ashley ground and gyrated her ass onto James' lap. James was careful to follow traditional strip club rule and kept his hands at his side.

"How about a private room dance Mr.?" Ashley asked.

"How much more will that cost?" James asked.

"Throw a couple more hundred down on the floor," Ashley said.

"How do I know it will be worth it?" James asked.

"If you have to ask all that, then maybe you're not man enough to find out," Ashley said as she licked her lips.

James looked his wife in her eyes ad dropped ten more twenty dollar bills on the floor.

"I'm worth it," Ashley said.

"Prove it," James demanded.

Ashley knelt on her knees in front of James unbuckled his belt, unzipped his pants and pulled them down along with his underwear. James was sitting with his head leaned back and looking up at the ceiling until he felt his wife's hot and moist breath on his sensitive excited manhood. James looked down at Ashley who gazed up at him as she accepted him into her warm mouth. The sight of Ashley pleasuring him while never taking her eyes away from his gaze was the most erotic things James had ever seen.

"My God Ashley. Suck that dick baby," James said as his hands touched her hair.

161

Ashley lowered James hands back down to his side and increased the speed of her motion. James had gripped the arms of the chair and was lifting his butt off the seat cushion to match Ashley's motion.

"Oh shit Ashley. That feels so fucking good baby," James said.

Ashley suddenly stopped and stood in front of James. James stared at his wife as she removed her panties and ran her fingers between her legs. Ashley then rubbed her fingers under James nose and across his lips.

"Don't I smell and taste good baby?" Ashley asked.

"You smell and taste great," James said.

"That was just a sample, now come and feast on the real thing," Ashley said as she stood facing James and placed her right foot on one arm of the chair. James leaned forward and buried his face into Ashley's smoldering valley of love.

"That's it baby, lick it just like that. Lick that hot, White pussy baby," Ashley said as she held on to the back of the chair for balance.

"Ohh!" Ashley uttered.

Ashley then turned her back to James, held her body up by holding onto the arms of the chair and then lowered herself until she felt James most exquisite intrusion. Ashley then moved her hips back and forth on James lap while also throwing in a rotating motion. James was in such a state of heightened arousal that he could not withstand the sensation.

"Goddamn baby. I'm coming! Ugnhh! Ugnhh!" James exclaimed.

"That's it! Give it to me! Ohhh fuck! Mmmm! That dick is so good baby! I love you James!" Ashley said as she fell backwards onto James in the chair.

James finally touched his wife and ran his hands over her sweat covered breasts as she sat on his lap with her head leaned back onto his shoulders.

"You're right. You were worth it," James said in gasps.

"Let's get one of these chairs when we get back home," Ashley said.

"That's a good idea," James said while still breathing heavily.

"I'll have you know I'm keeping all this money. You'll have to hit the ATM machine," Ashley informed James.

"I have no problem with that. It's half yours anyway," James replied.

That reward trip became one of James and Ashley's favorite adventures as they enjoyed many activities for the first time such as deep sea fishing and parasailing. On the last night before going home James and Ashley walked hand in hand along the dimly lit beach,

"James, I remember the first time I saw you. You were at band practice and had that tall hat on. You were tall and skinny. Then you did that move where you bent over backwards so far that the top of your hat touched the ground behind you. I thought to myself, now I could do something with that," Ashley laughed.

"I remember seeing you the first time when you were walking across campus wearing the tightest jeans I've ever seen in my life. I had all kind of thoughts running through my mind about what I could do with you," James said.

"My God, you have such a dirty mind," Ashley said.

"You know you love it," James said.

"What was that?" Ashley said as she heard a noise.

"I don't know. It sounded like a woman's voice," James said.

Ashley and James froze in their tracks before they heard the sound again. It was clearly a woman's voice and it sounded like she could be in distress. Up ahead of Jams and Ashley was one of the private cabanas that guests could reserve on the beach and the sound was coming from that direction.

"What do you want to do? Someone could be in trouble out here in the dark. There's no one else around except for us," Ashley said in a whisper.

"It's too far to go back to the hotel for help and if we yell who knows what will happen," James said.

James and Ashley stood until they heard what was definitely sounded like a woman in distress.

"I'm going over there and see what going on. Stay here," James whispered.

"No. I'm going with you," Ashley said quietly.

James saw a piece of driftwood in the sand and picked it up. With Ashley walking behind James they crept up to the side of the cabana. James activated a flashlight application on his phone and then stepped in front of the cabana. James pulled back the cloth covering the opening and the light from the phone lit up the interior of the cabana.

"Fuck me baby! What the fuck!" a woman's voice said.

"Venita!" James said in shock.

"Who the hell is there?! I can't see!" the man who was naked while lying between the legs of James sister said.

James quickly turned off the light and closed the covering to the cabana. It registered with Ashley that they had mistaken Venita's cries of sexual pleasure as sounds of distress. It was then crystal clear they interrupted Venita and Dashon's torrid lovemaking session out by the beach.

"Venita, we're so sorry. We heard a woman's voice and thought someone might be in trouble out here in the dark," Ashley said from outside the cabana.

"I'm so embarrassed. Ashley, you're not going to tell anyone in the company about this I could lose my job," Venita said from inside the enclosure.

"No, Venita, no, don't worry about that. I would never do that. We are leaving right now and giving you two your privacy. Sorry," Ashley said as she and James quickly walked away.

Finally Ashley and James got back to their room.

"Oh my God, I can't unsee what I saw tonight," James said.

"At least she was having a good time. He was packing," Ashley said with a laugh.

"Whatever. It's time to go home," James said as he fell backwards across the bed.

"Yes it is. I can't wait to see my baby. I miss Ashton so much," Ashley said.

15

Ashley felt so blessed once she was back at home in her normal routine. Every morning she looked at her husband, child and the home she shared with them almost in disbelief. Given where she came from it was difficult for Ashley to believe she was the same person living the same lifetime. There was such a distance between who she was compared to what she thought was possible for her when she was younger that it was almost a disconnection. Because of how she grew up, Ashley felt she didn't have a home base. Her parents never owned a home until she left for college and the trailer she grew up in was long gone and cattle grazed in the field where it once sat, but her son would not have that issue to deal with. Ashton had a home that he would be able to come back to when he got older and went away to find himself in the world. Ashley felt she and James had achieved the true American dream until the coldness of the world blasted its way into their reality.

James was on his way back from a company manager's meeting in Houston when he called Ashley.

"Baby I'm stopping by that barbeque joint in the south side and I'll bring home some of those baby back ribs you love so much. I'll be home soon. Ashley, I love you," James said.

"I love you too baby. See you soon," Ashley said.

"Ashton, your daddy will be home soon," Ashley said to her son who was sitting on her lap.

Ashley was waiting for James to arrive home and she thought that maybe something happened on the freeway and was holding him up. Ashley finally called James on his mobile phone and it rang before going to voicemail. Ashley began to worry. It should have taken James forty five minutes at the most to drive home from where the barbeque restaurant he stopped at to pick up a takeout meal. Ashley began to panic and called David one of James friends from work.

"David, this is Ashley. Have you heard from James?" Ashley asked.

"He called a few hours ago when he was still on his way from Houston, but not lately. Is something wrong?" David asked.

"I don't know. He called and said he was stopping to pick up some food at a barbeque place in south Dallas, you know the one we went to with you and Malika, but that was two hours ago. I'm getting really worried," Ashley said.

Right after Ashley made her statement a breaking news report interrupted the show that was on television about a police officer involved shooting. Ashley's eyes widened when the news helicopter camera zoomed in closer to the scene that had police vehicles surrounding a black Corvette in a liquor store parking lot.

"David! Oh my God! On television! That looks like James' car! Turn on channel eight! It's some kind of police shooting!" Ashley screamed.

"Ashley! We're coming over right now! It can't be James! Stay right there," David said.

Within thirty minutes. Ashley heard her doorbell ring. Ashley answered the door.

"Let's go! I know where that location is!" David said.

Ashley walked out of the door with Ashton in her arms. As they arrived close to the scene in the parking lot of the liquor store off Loop 12 in Dallas, Ashley's could see that the vehicle was James black Corvette Z06. Ashley ran up to the scene and was stopped by a uniformed officer.

"Where's my husband?!" Ashley screamed.

"Ma'am you have to stay back," The officer said.

"That's my husband's car! James Thomas is his name! I'm his wife Ashley!" Ashley screamed.

Malika stayed in the car with Aston so he wouldn't be frightened by the chaos at the scene.

"That car belongs to my friend James, this is his wife and we need to know what happened here!" David said.

A detective at the scene stepped forward.

"Mrs. Thomas, may I see your ID?" the detective asked.

Ashley showed her driver's license to the detective.

"Ma'am an incident took place here and one of our officers engaged your husband. An armed robbery took place nearby and one of our officers confronted Mr. Thomas because he fit the general description of the suspect. We don't know everything that happened, but our officer discharged her weapon as Mr. Thomas was seated in his vehicle. Mr. Thomas was transported to Parkland Hospital's emergency room," the detective informed.

All of the color drained from Ashley's face as she stood there in shock.

"What? You shot my James? Is he...?" Ashley asked before the detective answered.

"He's at the emergency room," the detective said.

"Are you fucking kidding me?! You think a man in a one hundred thousand dollar sports car and wearing a tie committed an armed robbery! Ashley let's get to the hospital!" David said.

Ashley did not know the man that robbed a convenience store was caught ten miles away when his car broke down on side of the road and he ran when a police cruiser stopped behind his vehicle. When the robber was caught, he still had a bag with store's logo printed on it filled with the money from the cash register in his possession. The perpetrator was a thirty four year old black man with a close haircut who was wearing a white shirt and driving an older model black Nissan 350Z two-seat sports car. Jawaun Hill had a long record of criminal activity and had the weapon used in the robbery in his possession. By the time Ashley arrived at the hospital emergency room the police department realized they had made a grievous mistake and the wrong man was in the hospital. Ashley ran into the emergency room and after telling the receptionist who she was, she was escorted to a surgery waiting room. A surgeon came in to the waiting room.

"Doctor, are you seeing after my husband?!" Ashley asked frantically.

"I'm Dr. Gipson. Are you Mrs. Thomas?" the doctor asked Malika who was holding Ashton.

"No, I'm Mrs. Thomas! I need to see my husband!" Ashley said as Dr. Gipson turned.

"I'm sorry Mrs. Thomas. Mr. Thomas is still in surgery. We are doing everything we can, but the bullet punctured his right lung. If we can stabilize him, he'll have a long way to go and will have to fight infections, but it's touch and go right now," Dr. Gipson said.

"Oh God! Can I see James? Please!" Ashley asked.

"Come with me. Mrs. Thomas only," Dr. Gipson said as he walked Ashley back to the door of the operating room.

Ashley looked through the window of the operating room door and saw what looked like a small army of medical professionals surrounding James body. Ashley looked on, but she couldn't see James' face due to it being shielded by a covering that blocked her view. Ashley wondered if she would ever see her husband alive again. Ashley then noticed a uniformed police officer stationed down from the operating room. The doctor led Ashley back to the waiting room. Ashley could not determine that the body on the operating table was her husband, James, since he was surrounded by a team of Doctors and nurses, plus hidden by coverings around every part of his body except where he was being operated on. Tears welled up in Ashley's eyes as the thought of losing James was too much to bear. The doctor led Ashley back to the waiting room where David, Malika and Ashton were stationed. Ashley collapsed into David and Malika's arms while Ashton was fast asleep on a sofa in the room.

"I need to call James' sisters and brother," Ashley said as she dialed Venita's phone number.

Ashley heard Venita scream in emotional pain over the phone when she told her what happened to James. Venita recovered enough to tell

Ashley she would call James' brother Joshua and his other sister Donita. Joshua was on the road in his big rig and just happened to be in Oklahoma. James dropped his load and immediately headed to Dallas. Venita dropped everything and began her drive from Shreveport to Dallas in the middle of the night. Donita and her husband got flights out as soon as they could the next morning to Texas so she could be there for her brother and Ashley. Everyone in the family was terrified about what could happen to James.

"Mrs. Thomas. Your husband survived the surgery, but he is heavily sedated and has been moved to a recovery room. Mr. Thomas is in critical condition and the next twenty four hours will be crucial. We have him on heavy doses of antibiotics to fight off potential infections from the damage to his lung. I'll bring you back so you can briefly see him in an isolation room. You will have to put on some protective clothing to lessen the chance of transmission of any infections given that his immunity is very low at this point," Dr. Gipson said.

Ashley eyes were as wide as they could be as the assessment given by the doctor brought the gravity of the situation into clear focus. Ashley simply nodded to indicate she understood and followed behind Dr. Gipson. Before she could proceed into the room with James, Ashley was outfitted in a protective gown, gloves and surgical mask. Ashley walked into the room that was a symphony of beeping, clicking and suction sounds as various pieces of medical equipment connected to James maintained his life.

Ashley was literally shaking as she took in the scene in front of her eyes. Digital displays of every aspect of James' bodily functions were all around his bed. Tubes and sensor wires attached to James body extended out in all directions and were a sobering confirmation to Ashley of how tenuous his grip was on life at that moment. Ashley advanced to the side of the bed and looked upon James face and could barely recognize him. James face was dark and swollen and he had a breathing tube in his mouth. A nurse was in the room, but she gave Ashley space while she monitored James vital signs.

"James, I know you can't hear me. It's me, Ashley. I'm here baby. I love you. Ashton is outside and he loves you too," Ashley said as she held James' right hand in her right hand and rubbed his cheek with her left hand. Ashley waited and hoped for some type of response from James, but none came. Tears began to run down Ashley's face.

"James, why did they do this to you? You never bothered anybody. Who do you have to be just to make it home to me safe and whole? I love you baby. I'm going to go now to see about our son,

but you have to make it home to me, please!"
Ashley said as she left the room.

Ashley looked back into the room at James
one more time as she walked away.

16

While Ashley was consumed by the personal tragedy that surrounded her family, a larger story was unfolding around them. News of the shooting of a Black Dallas business executive by a police officer had gained national attention. The outrage over how a man fitting a vague description of an armed robbery suspect was shot by a police officer while the actual perpetrator was caught miles away with the evidence and weapon used in the crime on his person was growing. Many were asking the same question Ashley verbalized at James bedside, but in different manner. One fed up Black man spoke into a television camera and crystallized the sentiment.

"Look, we're tired of this shit! Who the fuck do we have to be to keep from being shot by the police? He wasn't standing on the corner causing trouble or stealing something. He wasn't involved in some fight with the cops. This man had a tie on while he sat in his fancy sports car. Is there only supposed to be one Black man around driving a dark color two seat sports car? Come on man! What if the robber was a White man in a white pickup truck, are they going stop all of them too? This is fucked up! Then they caught the guy that did it and this other man is in the hospital fighting for his life! The guy that did it was driving a beat up old piece of shit, didn't have a tie on and his pants were sagging so bad he tripped trying to get away from the cops! What the fuck man?!" the man said.

By ten o'clock the next morning everyone had arrived and the news was everywhere. James' siblings as well as Ashley's parents and her brothers had arrived.

"Mama I never thought something like this could happen to James. I mean, he never did anything to anybody. James is a family man and works hard every day. What did he do to deserve this?" Ashley said as her mother held her.

"It's a mean world. People are scared of each other for no reason. I hate to say it, but it could have been a person that shouldn't have been a cop in the first place afraid of a Black man for no other reason than the color of his skin. I'm White, but I'm not blind to everything that's been going on around me," Katherine said.

"Look at what's on television!" Venita said.

"They're talking about James," Joshua said.

"Oh my God. It was a White woman cop that shot him," Donita said.

"She was suspended without pay. That doesn't happen that often. Without pay means they probably think she was in the wrong," Joshua speculated.

"I can't think about that right now. I'm worried about James," Ashley said.

"Mrs. Thomas, may I speak with you?" Dr. Asked as he came into the waiting room.

After speaking with the doctor, Ashley turned to everyone else in the room.

"James is more stable. They should be moving him to a regular room tomorrow," Ashley announced.

"Thank the lord!" Ashley's mother said.

"The Doctor said James still had a long way to go. Infections and the stress on his body have taken a toll on him. I need to take a shower and change clothes. I rented a room at a hotel around the corner, but all of my clothes are at home," Ashley said.

"Give me your keys and security code. We will go get some clothes for you. Just tell us what you need," Malika offered.

Ashley took Malika up on her offer and they went back to Ashley's home and gathered up clothes and other items for Ashley and Ashton. The waiting room became very busy as James' coworkers started coming by to check on him. James ran the Dallas operation for his company and what took place rippled through the organization nationwide. Ashley decided to leave the hospital briefly and was startled when she was surrounded by news reporters.

"Mrs. Thomas! Mrs. Thomas!" reporters shouted.

Joshua and Ashley's brother pushed through the throng of people so Ashley could be driven to the hotel to freshen up.

"What the hell is going on out here?!" Ashley's brother Ed Jr. asked.

"This has become a national story man with all these police shootings of Blacks that have been in the news. Since James seems to be the last person something like that should happen too, it's struck a nerve," Joshua said.

"I can't deal with all this right now. I just want James to be okay," Ashley said as she looked at all the faces outside the vehicle's window.

Once she was back at the hospital, Ashley ordered a bed for James hospital room so she could sleep there and not leave his side. Ashley was walled off from the world as anger and outrage grew around them on the outside. What people involved in various movements, politicians and talking heads on cable news stations thought about what happened to James meant nothing to Ashley at that time. An overwhelming sense of sadness fell over her as she listened to the relentless sounds of the medical equipment that never ceased. Various family members came and went, but Ashley never left James side again. On the third day Ashley was standing at James bedside wiping his forehead with a wet towel while she held his hand and something almost miraculous happened, Ashley felt James squeeze her hand.

"James! Baby can you hear me?" Ashley asked.

James couldn't speak, but he squeezed Ashley's hand again. Ashley looked at James' face and his eyelids fluttered.

"Oh my God!"Ashley said as she pressed a button to call a nurse.

A nurse ran into the room and asked if something had happened.

"James squeezed my hand and his eyelids moved!" Ashley said excitedly.

The nurse checked James' vital signs and Dr. Gipson came in and looked into his eyes.

"It looks like his body is responding to the antibiotics and we decreased the dose of drugs that kept your husband in a near medically induced coma. He's responding, but we will take it slow by decreasing the dose daily to allow increased neurological activity, but we still need to handle the pain a trauma like what happened to your husband causes to the human body. It helps that your husband was a very fit person when this happened," Dr. Gipson said.

"Dr. Gipson, will my husband make it? Will he live?" Ashley asked.

"We are doing everything we can, but as much as we can do with medical science, we are not miracle workers. Right now it's up to us to make sure we do all we can to put your husband in the best possible position to survive this tragedy, but nature has to play its role in this process as well. We are doing all we can," Dr. Gipson said as he left the room.

Ashley felt empty inside because she thought the doctor would be more optimistic and tell her everything would be fine, but he didn't. Ashley prepared herself for both the best and worst of possible outcomes. Life without James didn't seem possible, but given she was in a situation she never dreamed of a week earlier proved to her that life could take her in directions she never imagined. Ashley sat down next to James and held his hand.

"James, I've loved you since I first laid eyes on you. I don't want to lose you, but if you can't come back to me, I know it's not what you wanted to happen. You shouldn't be here, but God does things we can't understand. Our son hasn't seen you since all this happened and he's asking about you all the time, he wants his daddy. I want his daddy too," Ashley said through tears.

"Ashley," James said weakly in the faintest whisper.

"What? James did you say something?" Ashley said as she stood and placed her face close to James mouth.

"Ashley," James said again at an almost inaudible volume.

"James, you spoke!" Ashley said but James went back into his drug induced unconsciousness.

Ashley walked out of the hospital and walked up to the police officer standing down from James' hospital room.

"Why are you here?! You caught the man that robbed that store, so why are you here?! Ashley asked.

"Ma'am, I'm just doing my job," the officer replied.

Ashley looked at the officer and walked away. Ashley went to the waiting room and told everyone that James tried to talk, but also relayed what the doctor told her. Three days later Ashley thought everything had turned around when James called her name in a surprisingly strong voice.

"Ashley," James said in the middle of the night.

"James, I'm here baby," Ashley said.

"She shot me," James said as he lay still in his bed.

"I know baby. I know," Ashley said.

"Why?" James questioned.

"I don't know," Ashley said.

"I didn't do anything," James said.

"I know you didn't," Ashley said.

"I didn't do anything," James said before dropping off to sleep.

Ashley went to her bed and the exhaustion of being constantly under stress for days caused her to drift off to sleep and dream of the good times she shared with James over the years. The next day James was more alert and recognized Ashley, Ashton and his siblings. The police officer that was posted near James room was no longer there because there was no basis to file charges against James after a review of the officer that shot James body camera video. James managed a slight smile when he saw Ashton.

"Give daddy a kiss on the cheek," Ashley said as she held Ashton in a position so e could kiss his father.

"How do you feel James?" Venita asked.

"I hurt everywhere. It hurts to breath," James said with a pained expression on his face.

"Why was I shot?" James asked softly.

Ashley explained what she had been told by the police and what she heard on news reports.

"They caught the guy, but she shot me?" James said puzzled.

"James, I'm so sorry, but she's not going to get away with what she did to you, but I want you to get well and come home first. After you get out of here we will make them pay for what happened to you," Ashley said.

Ashley looked over at James' family and when she turned around James was sound asleep.

"I guess his body still needs a lot of rest," Ashley said to Donita.

"I don't know what to do. I mean James is awake and talking, but he seems so weak. I need to get back to work, but I don't want to leave him like this," Donita said through tears.

"Donita, I understand that you can't stay here forever, so don't feel guilty if you need to go home to keep your job. I understand and James would understand that too," Ashley said.

"I know, but I don't want to leave, but I have to. I'll be back on the weekend. I know James is going to make it. He has to," Donita said through tears.

"Look everybody, I know you all can't stay here as long as I can, so don't risk losing you jobs. I'll be here. My mother will still be here. Even my dad has to go back home because of his job. None of us are rich and can just stop everything forever, even for something like this. I understand," Ashley said.

"We'll I'm staying as long as I can. I'll miss some loads, but I'm good for a while. That's my little brother laying over there," Joshua said.

Within two days Ashley found she was standing a lonely vigil by James bedside. Visits by Ashley's mother, Joshua, James coworkers and

184

friends interrupted her solitary watch, but she was a constant presence. Ashley also became concerned that James recovery seemed to be standing still and she was not able to understand fully why he was not getting better. Then one morning Ashley woke up and James was breathing in a labored fashion.

"James," Ashley said as she walked up next to him.

Ashley felt James forehead and he felt cold.

"Oh my God!' Ashley eclaimed.

Ashley bolted from the room and called for help.

"Nurse! Nurse! Something's wrong with my husband!" Ashley yelled.

A nurse ran from the nurse's station down to James' room. The nurse checked James' vital signed and listened to his lungs. The nurse put out a call for help to come to James room. The on-duty doctor came into the room and after examining James he walked over to Ashley.

"Mrs. Thomas, You husband has developed pneumonia in his right lung. We will place him on a regimen of strong antibiotics, but his body is under tremendous stress," the doctor said.

James health declined slowly over the next two days to the point that a breathing tube was inserted back into James mouth.

"Mrs. Thomas, I think you may want to call your family. Things are cascading with your husband. His immune system is low and his heart is failing. The pneumonia has spread to his healthy lung as well as the compromised lung," Dr. Gipson said.

"Doctor, are you telling me my husband is dying?! I thought he was getting better. James was talking a few days ago. How could this be happening?" Ashley said as she sat down in a chair and wept.

"I have to ask you something very important. If something happens to Mr. Thomas, do you want us to take extraordinary measures to keep him alive?" Dr. Gipson asked.

"You mean like life support and feeding tubes?" Ashley asked.

"Yes ma'am," Dr. Gipson said.

"No. James said he lived like a man and wanted to die like a man. James didn't want our son to see him waste away. If God decides James has to leave this world, he will leave with dignity," Ashley said.

Two days later James was surrounded by family and he had no wires or tubes connected to his body except for an intravenous drip to control pain. James breathing was shallow and his eyes were set and not moving.

"James!" Ashley said as James breaths slowed and became father apart.

Then James took one last exhale and never inhaled again.

"James, no!" Ashley screamed as she threw herself across her husband's lifeless body.

Tears flowed from every eye in the room as no one could believe James, a husband, father and brother was gone for unexplainable reasons. Ashley felt totally empty inside and knew her life would never be the same again. Ashton was in the waiting room with Janika and Ashley feared as he grew older, he would not remember his father.

The grim process of James' body moving from the hospital to the coroner played out and an autopsy would be performed, but there was not an open question to be answered. James Thomas was a healthy and vibrant man before being shot in the chest by a police officer and all other complications that lead to his untimely death revolved around that reality.

17

It was two o'clock in the afternoon on a Monday and Ashley finally left the hospital and went home with her mother and son. On Wednesday morning Ashley Thomas was sitting on a sofa flanked by the CEO of Infostream Software, Inc., James former employer, and one of the most famous criminal lawyers in the nation, Marshall Moskowitz. Joining them was civil rights legend, Congressman Jonathan Davis. Mel Loftin, the cohost of Good Day America, the top morning news show in the nation, was conducting the interview and introduced the assembled group to the viewing audience.

"Mrs. Thomas, first of all you have our condolences for the loss of your husband James in this tragic manner," Mel said.

"Thank you Mel," Ashley said.

"Almost two weeks ago your husband was confronted by a uniformed police officer in the parking lot of a liquor store after he bought a bottle of your favorite wine to bring home for dinner. The officer's official account of what happened was that he fit the description of a robbery suspect and that is why he was approached. What do you think about her account?" Mel asked Ashley.

"I don't think much of it. Was there only one Black man out there driving a dark color, two seat sports car? There was no exact color given by the witness, no make or year model. Was it an older or newer model car, nothing. Why would a person who just committed armed robbery stop at a liquor store, of all places, next to one of the busiest highways in the entire city? None of it makes any sense. My husband was a businessman with a white dress shirt and necktie on while he was sitting in a one hundred thousand dollar sports car. Mel, tell me just who does a Black man have to be to keep from getting killed by cops that shouldn't be on the streets?" Ashley said.

"Mel, that's the whole point of us being here. James Thomas was the American dream. He was the first in his family to go to college. He rose to a prominent position of responsibility in one of the largest technology companies in the country. He was a husband and father. We want every Black man to be a James Thomas and still, when it came down to it, he was seen as being just another scary Black man and taken out by a cop with what I believe was an irrational fear of Black men. This has to stop and stop now, because we are tired of it," Congressman Davis said.

Mel, then directed a question at Richard Wilson, the President and CEO of Infostream Software, Incorporated.

"Mr. Wilson, James Thomas was a manager for your company. Why do you feel it's important for you to be here?" Mel asked.

"James was an important and respected member of our management team. James was part of the Infostream family. He was coming home from a management meeting in Houston when this happened. I considered James to still be on the job when that happened, because he had not made it home from a company directed business meeting.

I had met Ashley before at two of our recognition events we have on an annual basis. More important than any of the prior things I have mentioned, James was a good man, a loving husband and father. We are a large organization and seek the best people out without regard to race or gender. I understand that law enforcement has a tough job to do and every day they know there is the possibility that they may not make it back home. Police officers are sworn to protect and serve everyone and that can't happen if one group among us is looked upon as being inherently dangerous and often met with deadly force. How do we manage to arrest a bomber who had a shootout with the police in New Jersey alive and a Black man who did nothing and was trying to make it home ends up dead at the hands of a cop? I didn't want to believe what was being said about inherent racial bias among some in law enforcement, but then it came to my front door. James Thomas will not die in vain and the full weight of Infostream Software, Inc. is behind making a change in what is happening to

Black citizens at the hands of bad cops and also to assist police departments weed out people that shouldn't be in the job," Wilson said.

"Isn't it a risky move for a company to take a public stance on a controversial topic like this?" Mel asked.

"Mel, that's where you're wrong. This is not a topic. This is reality. Ashley's husband, James Thomas, was killed at the hands of a police officer for what seems to be no reason at all. Over the years countless other African American's have died over the years at the hands of cops under circumstances that didn't seem to warrant the use of deadly force. Now many of these incidents have been caught on camera so we all get to see what went on. You have a point, why is my company getting involved. I am a student of history and Dr. Martin Luther King, Jr. wrote in his book, Strength to Love, and I wrote this down:

'The ultimate measure of a man is not where he stands in moments of comfort and convenience, but where he stands at times of challenge and controversy. The true neighbor will risk his position, his prestige, and even his life for the welfare of others.'

So Mel, it's time for those of us who are comfortable to risk something for our neighbor's welfare. James wasn't just an employee of this company he was my neighbor. I don't have to look like James to do something. James' wife doesn't have to be the same ethnicity as her husband who was taken from her to do something. If athletes can take a knee to bring attention to this issue, I can go one step further," Wilson said.

"Well said sir. Mr. Moskowitz, you have been involved on some of the most high profile trials in the last fifty years in this country's history. You were in semi-retirement, why did you decide to take this on," Mel asked.

"Well, my friend Richard called me and told me about James Thomas. I had been keeping up with what was going on television, but if it meant something to Richard, it meant something to me. He told me that it was time for me to leave a mark on history and address what has been going on with what seems to be a disproportionate early use of deadly force against African Americans without justifiable threat of danger. That is what this is all about. We have not viewed the police dashcam and body camera video, but we will see that tomorrow at Dallas police headquarters. It's ironic that this happened in a city with one of the best community policing programs in the nation, but this officer came from another area before joining the force and it appears she had problems where she came from that were not reported to Dallas before she joined their department. After we see the video, it will be release to the public," Moskowitz said.

"That's new information. Ashley I'll let you have the last words here today," Mel said.

"I just want to thank everyone for their support. I have received so many social media messages of support and I thank all of you for that. I will see how my husband died when I watch those videos tomorrow, so I need your prayers for strength and for our son who will never see his father again. Regardless of what comes out when those videos go public, I want peace, not violence. James wouldn't want anyone else to get hurt because of what happened to him. I will bury my husband on Saturday and I want to ask all those people sending mean, hateful and racist messages to me because my husband was Black and I'm White, what kind of soul do you have? What Bible do you read that tells you to hate my late husband because of the color of his skin and hate me because of who I loved. You've even called our son all kind of names because his parents were of different races. I loved my husband and yes he was a Black man and I'm a White woman! Most of you can't look in the mirror and say you're half the person my husband James was. Shame on you, except you have no shame and hide behind the internet with fake user names spewing racial hate! You're a bunch of cowards!" Ashley said through tears.

Ashley didn't know that the camera had zoomed in on her face and broadcast her tearful and pained facial expression to the entire nation. That moment was broadcast and replayed countless times on television and social media. Ashley Thomas became a household name for her passionate defense of her deceased husband James. The following day, Ashley along with James' siblings and Attorney Marshall Moskowitz watched the dashcam and then body camera video.

"There's James getting into his car with something in his right hand. Oh my God! She jumped out of her car with her gun drawn! She's running up to James' driver's side window," James sister Donita said as she watched.

"Drop it! Don't move!" the officer yelled.

"Officer what's the problem? I just have a…" James could be heard saying.

"Bang!" as a gunshot sounded.

"Oh shit! That's when she shot him! That was less than a minute from the time she jumped out of the police car! What the fuck!" Joshua said.

"Shots fired! Shots fired!" The officer said as she called for assistance.

The body camera video was shown next and it broke Ashley's heart along with those of the rest of his family. The video showed the officer run up to James' car with her gun in her hands pointing toward James.

"Drop it! Don't move!" The officer yelled.

It was clear that James was surprised at the officer being there and his face was shown clearly in the video.

"James," Ashley said as she reached toward the television screen.

"Officer what's the problem? I just have a…" James said as he reached toward an object in the passenger seat.

"Bang!" the sound of a gunshot rang out.

"Oh Jesus! She just shot James!" Ashley said as she turned her head and Venita held her.

James' head jerked around in the direction of the camera and his left hand touched the right side of his chest. James looked at his hand covered in blood.

"Why did you shoot me?" James said softly.

"Shots fired! Shots fired!" the officer said.

The video ended and police chief stepped into the viewing room.

"Mrs. Thomas. I want to let you know that you and Mr. Thomas family have our condolences for the loss of your husband. There was no weapon on your husband's person or in his vehicle. The object in the passenger seat was a bottle of wine he had just purchased from the liquor store. Officer Sherry Morris has been relieved of her duties and is no longer a member of the Dallas Police Department. This case has been referred to a grand jury for consideration of whatever charges are deemed appropriate in this situation. As you know we apprehended the robbery suspect in the incident that caused your husband to come under suspicion. Again you have our deepest sympathies," the chief said again.

"She murdered my husband! Your officer murdered James!" Ashley said in rage as Joshua grabbed her as she lunged toward the chief of police.

The chief dropped his head and left the room. Ashley broke down in tears and sobbed while sitting on the floor of the room they were in. The next day, the videos James' loved ones saw in private was released to the public. Reaction was swift and calls for murder charges against the officer that shot James came in from all corners of the nation.

Seeing the moment James was shot had a profound effect upon Ashley. Everything seemed real and fresh, but still unbelievable that something like what happened took the love of her life away from her and Ashton. Ashley wondered how she would get through the funeral she never imagined three weeks before. Ashley had made a bold move earlier when planning James' services. Seated behind the family would be the mothers of other African Americans that died at the hands of police officers and other racially motivated gun violence over the last few years. Protesters gathered in major cities all over the country the night after videos of James' shooting were broadcast. One Black teenager was asked what he thought about what happened to James and he gave a sobering response.

"People always said you need to stay out of trouble, get a good education and a good job to be successful. James Thomas did all that and the police still killed him because he was Black. It was like it didn't matter man. I guess she was scared of him or something and shot him for no reason. I'm scared of the police. It's like they can just shoot you for nothing," the boy said.

The words spoken by that Black youth rippled through the Black community because it signaled a line of thinking that was becoming imbedded into generations of the future. If young African Americans began to believe that achievement doesn't matter in the end, because they could still be taken out by a cop with bad judgment or irrational fear of African Americans. Leaders in the Black community knew they didn't need additional reasons for young Blacks to avoid pursuing higher education and professional success.

Ashley was trying to shut out the outside world as she prepared to lay her husband to rest. One day ahead of the funeral services and before James' wake on a Friday night, Ashley was told someone called for her on Venita's phone. Venita walked up to Ashley.

"Who is it? Who would call for me on your phone?" Ashley asked.

"I think you should take this call in private," Venita said.

Ashley took the phone and went into the master bedroom.

"Hello, this is Ashley Thomas. Who is this," Ashley asked.

"This is Shenita Thomas, James' ex-wife. I know you don't know me and I hope you are not offended by me calling you at a time like this, but I wanted to speak with you convey my sympathy. I know things ended badly between James and me, but he was a good man. It broke my heart to see what that cop did to him. I'm sorry for your loss and I'm praying for you and your son," Shenita said.

"Thank you and no, I'm not offended by your call. Thank you," Ashley said.

"You're welcome and I wish you well," Shenita said as the call ended.

It was Saturday morning and James funeral service started at noon in one of the largest megachurches in Dallas. Ashley sat in her bedroom seated on the edge of the bed when a knock came at the door.

"Come in," Ashley said.

Ashley's mother walked into the room.

"Ashley, are you doing okay?" Katherine asked.

"No mama, I'm not doing okay. I hate funerals and now I have to sit on the front row at my husband's funeral. It was hard enough at the wake last night. I touched James' face. It was so hard and cold. He's gone, isn't he?" Ashley said.

"Yes baby, he's gone. I know he loved you. James told me how lucky he was to get a second chance with you and how you gave him a beautiful son. He was so happy with his life because of you," Katherine said.

"James told you that? I don't understand why God allows things like this to happen to good people. I keep feeling like James will walk into the house through the door that leads to the garage like he did every night he came home from work, but he won't," Ashley said before beginning to sob.

"Honey we can question God, but we can't understand his ways and motivations. It could be that there is a higher purpose for James' life that will be achieved through his death. It could be that it's up to those he left behind to make that happen," Katherine said.

"Maybe you're right. I won't let James' death be meaningless, but mama I miss him so much," Ashley said as she fell into her mother's arms.

Three hours later Ashley found herself sitting on the front row inside the massive sanctuary of The First Redeemer Church with James' flower covered coffin positioned in front of the pulpit. Ashley felt like she wasn't quite sure how she came to be sitting where she was at that moment. Ashley sat there knowing the nation was watching as she consented to allow James' services to be broadcast live for television viewing.

Ashley sat there with her young son by her side. Ashley wore a black dress that came to her knees, a gold broach and black hat with a black lace veil that covered her face. Sitting in the row behind Ashley were seven mothers of African Americans that died at the hand of police officers or gun violence under questionable justification for the use of deadly force. Ashley's mind was in a fog as she listened to different speakers, singers and preachers speak eloquently about her deceased husband. Ashley did not sit silently throughout the service, but she got up and walked to the pulpit and lifted the veil that covered her face. Those assembled in the sanctuary seemed to hold their breaths in anticipation of what Ashley would say.

"I want to let everyone know that I would give the world to not be here today, but at home with my husband and son. My life and the life of my son were changed forever when a police officer decided James Thomas was so dangerous while just

200

sitting in his car that she had to shoot him. My husband fought for his life, but lost the battle. We never thought this horror that has been visiting families all over this country would touch us. We didn't live in a high crime area, we didn't hang out with people prone to attract the attention of the police and we didn't engage in criminal activities. My husband was a hard working family man. James Thomas was the head of our household, a loving husband and great father to our son. We were two professionals living the American dream, but unfortunately when James was out in the world away from home, some saw him differently than I did. That perception of James as a Black man by some who had some implicit fear in their hearts in general made him vulnerable if he encountered the wrong person with a weapon and it finally happened. Irrational fear of my strong, but gentle husband, because his skin was black. That's the only explanation I can find, because even if James fit some general description of someone that committed a crime. It would have taken a very brief amount of time to determine he had nothing to do with an armed robbery, if he had been approach like a real American, you know, innocent until proven guilty. No, my husband was treated like so many African Americans, guilty, but without a chance to be proven innocent, because he is dead now at the hands of an executioner wearing a uniform indicating she was sworn to serve and protect him, not kill him. Now I stand here, just like those mothers sitting in the row of seats behind me, would you all stand, who lost their children to gun violence from police officers and those harboring hate and fear in their hearts for people of color. Now here I stand and I know I look different than those mothers sitting behind me because of the color of my skin, but love doesn't know color, love only knows your heart. That officer broke my heart and took my love away from me. I have watched so many of these memorials on television and usually they never show the image of the loved one that was lost and I know that is a personal choice of the families left behind, but I feel differently. It's like a war is going on but we never see the fallen one last time, so it doesn't feel quite as real," Ashley said and stretched out her right hand.

The funeral directors marched down to the front of the sanctuary, removed the flowers from the coffin and open the top to reveal the upper torso of James' body for viewing.

"There he is, my husband James Thomas, my everything. He is wearing the tie I bought as a Christmas gift and it is the same tie he was wearing when he was shot by that police officer. I know his spirit is gone, but James will not die in vain, I won't allow it. I felt it was important for everyone to see that this is the result of the insanity that has been going on between the Black community and the police. This is when I realized the Black community is not about where you live, but about who you are, because even if you don't physically live in what is considered a Black community, it lives in you, because if you are Black, like my husband was, your address has no bearing on how you will be perceived out in the world. James Thomas was a great example of a man and he is a testimony to that reality, as tragic as it is. Thank you all for being here and thank you for all your prayers," Ashley said as she took her seat.

The officiating minister walked up to the pulpit and directed the funeral directors to initiate the process of allowing everyone there to walk by the coffin for on last viewing of James' body. The last group to view James body was his immediate family. James two sisters had to be helped back to their seats as they almost collapsed while standing before the body of their deceased younger brother. Finally Ashley walked up to the coffin with Ashton in her arms flanked by her mother and father. Ashley stood there in silence before leaning over and placing a soft kiss on the forehead of James' body. James would be lowered into his grave with a perfect red imprint of his beloved wife's lips on his forehead. Before they went back to their seats, Ashton made on final determination.

"Mama, Daddy's sleep," Ashton surmised.

"Yes baby, your daddy is asleep," Ashley said as tears started to stream down her face. Edward grabbed his daughter around her shoulders to support her while her mother took Ashton in her arms when they noticed Ashley's knees buckle when she turned to walk back to her seat.

Finally the services were over as everyone marched out of the church behind James' coffin that was hoisted high on the shoulders of six casket bearers walking in synchronized goose steps down the church aisle. After leaving the grave Ashley had the feeling that she was now truly alone with her son. Although James was already dead, the finality of burial made it real because she could never look upon his face again the flesh. The three dimensional James she knew and his love was gone forever in the flesh in any form, dead or alive. Now the period of truly missing him and living with her husband as a memory began, but there was much work to do that would keep her busy.

18

A grand jury indicted the police officer that shot James on manslaughter charges and she was arrested. Ashley pulled up her mugshot and gasped. Officer Sherry Morris looked like some kind of glamour model in her mugshot with long blonde hair, meticulous makeup and red lipstick. Morris was thirty two years old and had been a Dallas police officer for three years after starting her career in law enforcement in a mid-sized city in Arizona. It appeared that Morris had a reputation for being extremely tough on Hispanic residents in her prior position and had amassed reprimands that were not provided to the Dallas Police Department when her background was checked before she joined the force. Morris' relationships with police officials in her prior department caused them to omit detrimental details about her prior violations when she sought employment with the Dallas Police Department. Ashley's phone received an incoming call.

"Hi Venita, what's up," Ashley said.

"I'm just checking on you. Did you see the mugshot of the cop that shot James?" Venita said.

"Yes, I just looked at it. Who takes a mugshot like that after being indicted for manslaughter? She's smiling and everything. What a bitch!" Ashley said.

"I know what she's doing and she does too. She's playing up the big scary Black man versus the pure blonde White woman bullshit, but she was the one with a gun. You know how it is when it a good looking White woman is involved. That bitch better not get away with killing my brother just because the men involved in investigating this want to fuck her!" Venita said angrily.

"Venita, I don't how she looks or what kind of 'I thought he had a gun' story she tells. I'm going to try and send her ass to prison for shooting James for no reason. I know all about the Emmit Till situation and many others like it. She's not going to be able to pull that shit on us and get away with it. Don't worry," Ashley said.

"Ashley, you're the blackest White woman I know. I'm proud to have you as my sister-in-law. James loved him some Ashley. He was ready to whup my ass over you when we first met, I said damn, what has this woman put on my little brother. I miss him so much," Venita said.

"I do to. I still reach for James at night, but he's not there. It hurts. Ashton is still waiting for his daddy to come home. I told him James is in heaven, but he's too young to understand that. We have to make sure James' name stays alive and we do something to help stop this madness. Thanks for calling Venita. I'll talk to you later," Ashley said.

Ashley never returned to her job after James was shot. James, being the responsible man he was, had taken out a two million dollar life insurance policy on himself when he found out she was pregnant with their son. Ashley kept up her close friendship with Janeka, but the mothers' of the other Black men and women killed by police or gun violence became an important support system for her. Ashley found herself involved in efforts to bring awareness to the issue of distrust between the Black community and police. As with many of the other police involved shootings the public outcry over James' death came and went after a few marches and rallies, but Ashley and her team were just getting started.

Ashley's attorney, Marshall Moskowitz, took a novel approach. Not only did he approach they police department, he also went to where he thought the real problem rested, the police unions. Moskowitz said one of the problems with getting problem officers off the street, was keeping them off the police force permanently. In his research Moskowitz found that officers fired for various department violations were often quietly reinstated with back pay once their police officers union became involved. Moskowitz wanted to bring the issue of how difficult it was to weed out unfit officers when they were back on the force due to the strength of their police officer's union into the forefront. With the help of Ashley, the mothers of Blacks killed unjustly by police and the resources of James' former employer a campaign was launch to literally shame the police unions to change their ways. Ads began to run on television featuring the profile of officers and the infractions they were fired for with the result being them getting their jobs back due to intervention by their police union. The names of the officers were never mentioned and the issues concentrated on were those involving charges of excessive use of force, racial targeting and sexual abuse or bias. The ads featured the mothers of those lost to police violence. Ashley did not appear in an ad due to the pending trial of the officer that shot James.

Bail was set at one million dollars for Officer Morris and she did not have the resources to post a bond to get out of jail, but due to a funding account set up by her supporters she was able to walk out of jail pending trial. Morris had become somewhat of an internet sensation and was labeled the cutie cop.

Morris was blond and beautiful, but she was no shrinking violet. Morris stood five feet eight inches tall, had a chiseled body from weightlifting and rode a custom chopper when she was off duty. With tattoos on her shoulders and thighs she became a morbid media sensation when her social media photos made their rounds on the internet. The image of Morris that seemed to be everywhere was one with Morris sitting astride her chromed motorcycle wearing a bikini, heels and a police hat. Morris was leaned forward in the photo wearing red lipstick with her lips slightly open and her tongue sticking out, but barely visible. Morris took the photo long before her encounter with James and posted it on her social media accounts. Before Morris was advised to take the racy image down it was copied and distributed everywhere.

Ashley was furious over the flood of attention directed at her husband's killer. Social media was ablaze with all manner of cruel comments referring to James as an uppity nigger who was put in his place by the cutie cop. Ashley was incensed that a Black man that started with nothing and worked hard to get where he was in life was referred to as an uppity nigger instead of a successful American enjoying the fruits of his labor. Ashley wondered why a successful Black man driving a sports or luxury automobile was called cocky, a showboat or uppity when a White person driving the same vehicle was a sports car enthusiast or simply successful. Ashley thought back on when she and James sat on that curb in handcuffs while cops searched their SUV in Shreveport because Trevor called his police friend with a false story motivated by his anger at seeing James with a White woman as his fiancée. Ashley was shaken out of her reflective mood when Ashton ran into the room after waking up from his nap.

For her part, Sherry Morris tried to keep a lower profile publicly. Although she was beloved by a growing group of supporters, Sherry knew her life as she knew it was on the line. Sherry knew she could spend from two to twenty years in prison if found guilty. Sherry's attorney told her that her glamour mugshot was a mistake that appeared to make light of a life lost at her hands.

For three months Ashley occupied herself with the campaign to make changes in how bad cops were processed out of police forces and the union intervention back door that allowed them back onto police forces nationwide. Ashley's phone received an incoming call and it was her attorney telling her a date had been set for the trial of Sherry Morris to begin. Ashley felt a rush of nerves as she would have to relive the horrible experiences that surrounded James eventual death from being shot by former police officer Sherry Morris during a trial. The closer the trial date approached the more Ashley's dread of the process increased.

The time for the trial to begin was closing in, but jury selection took two weeks. Finally the jury was selected and seated. Three African American men, four African American women, one

Hispanic woman and four White men comprised the panel. Before deliberations began, Sherry Morris agreed to a plea deal. Advised by her legal counsel that the makeup of the jury may not lead to a favorable outcome, Morris plead guilty to manslaughter in exchange for a sentence of five years in prison The one stipulation for Morris was there would not be an opportunity for early parole.

Ashley felt both relief and rage at the same time. Ashley felt guilty for agreeing to the plea deal offer when her attorney brought it to her attention, but that put an end to that part of the saga. Ashley watched as Sherry Morris stood, was handcuffed and lead away. Morris turned and looked at Ashley.

"I'm sorry!" Morris said as she was lead away.

"Go to hell bitch!" Ashley yelled back at Morris.

"Mrs. Thomas! Another outburst like that and I'll find you in contempt of court. This court is dismissed," the judge shouted as he slammed his gavel down.

One year after the unexpected end of Sherry Morris' trial for James death, Ashley achieved a breakthrough. The largest police union in the nation signed an agreement with multiple major city police departments to honor the James Thomas agreement. The James Thomas agreement meant that after an initial review if it was proved that an officer's firing for excessive force, racial bias or sexual bias or abuse was valid, the union would not use extraordinary appeals to restore that individual back to the force.

Ashley and the mothers of Blacks lost to police or gun violence were all present when the Dallas Police Department and the head of the largest police union signed the agreement. As Ashley left the event a national television reporter stopped her.

"Mrs. Thomas. I know this has been a long effort, but some people don't understand why this agreement will make a difference," the reporter said.

"Well one of the issues we deal with in the area of these tragic events is that it is not often that an entire police department has problems with their relationships with the Black community, but a few officers that have poor judgment or inherent bias. What this agreement does is to try and remove police officers with bad records from police departments before something tragic happens and keep them from coming back. This will not keep all future tragedies from happenings, but if officers know that it's not a boomerang situation if they are fired for the particular issues in the agreement, then maybe it will cause some of them to be a little more cognizant of treating citizens of all races and sexual orientation the same when they encounter them. It's a start and better training is also important," Ashley said.

"Some are calling you the new face of action to stop unjustified police violence against Blacks," the reporter said.

"I'm not the face of anything. The face of this movement is my husband James' face and the faces of the lost love ones of those mothers that were on stage with me. The faces of this movement are all the Blacks taken away over the years before there were cameras around to record their fates. What is going on now is not new, it's just captured on video and televised," Ashley said as she walked away.

Before she went home, Ashley stopped by James' grave.

"James, I miss you baby. We got something done today. It was a small step, but we got something done. Ashton is in preschool now and he is so smart. You would be so proud of him. I love you and will love you forever," Ashley said before she left.

20

After Ashley arrived back at home she had an unexpected visitor knock on her door a few hours later.

"Venita! What are you doing here?" Ashley said.

"I saw you on television and had to come see about you," Venita said as she sat down.

"It's good to see you," Ashley said.

"Where's Ashton?" Venita asked.

"He's spending the night with his little friend Chad from preschool, so I have the house to myself," Ashley said.

"Oh, I'm sorry. I hope I'm not interrupting anything," Venita said.

"Interrupting anything, like what?" Ashley asked while looking puzzled.

"You could have a man over here," Venita said.

"A man! Are you serious?" Ashley said.

"Why did you respond like that? Ashley, do you mean you aren't seeing anybody?" Venita said.

"No, I'm not. I've been so wrapped up with the trial, and then trying to get this agreement pushed through, plus with Ashton, I haven't even thought about a man. I almost can't imagine another man touching me, other than James," Ashley said.

"Ashley, James was my brother, but he's been gone for a long time. What about what your need as a woman?" Venita asked.

"I haven't felt like a woman in a long time. I've felt like a widow, a mother and a crusader for a cause. How would I even fit a man in my life and bring him around my son?" Ashley said.

"Ashley, do you remember what you asked me one day when you were down there for my mother's funeral?" Venita asked.

"What did I ask? I don't remember," Ashley said.

"You asked how long people in my family lived and told me with all those years I had left to live I could change my life and find a man that would be worthy of me. You can do the same thing," Venita said.

"How do I let James go? He was the last man to touch me that way. Even though he's been gone so long, I would feel like I was cheating on him by being with someone else. James didn't walk out on me or leave me for another woman, he was taken from me by that cop shooting him," Ashley said.

"I know, I know, but Ashley, James is not coming back and he wouldn't want you to be alone," Venita said.

"I know and I'm so scared. I don't want to mess up and bring a man around that would be mean to Ashton. James brought us this far, but he's gone and can't be with us to the end. I feel so betrayed by God. My husband is gone forever and the woman that killed him is alive in prison. She will get out and continue her life, but look at what she did to us," Ashley said with tears streaming down her face.

Venita let Ashley cry into her shoulder and then took a tissue and dried her tears.

"I'm sorry," Ashley apologized.

"It's okay. You needed to get that out, but I know what we need to do. Ashley, go put on something nice. This is Friday night. You are getting out of this house and going out on the town with your sister-in-law. Aston is sleeping over with his friend, so you have no excuse," Venita said.

Ashley looked at Venita for a long time before speaking.

"Okay. It has been a long time since I just went out and had some fun," Ashley said as she stood.

Thirty minutes later Ashley came back out wearing a form fitting and mid-thigh length black dress. Ashley finished off her looks with a pair of five inch heels.

"What do you think?" Ashley said.

"I think you look great, but there is one thing you need to change," Venita said.

"Is it my hair?" Ashley asked.

"No, it's your wedding ring," Venita said.

"My wedding ring, but I always wear it everywhere," Ashley said.

"I know you do, but that part of your life is over now. I loved James too. He was my brother and he will always be my brother whether he is here or not, but he can't be your husband anymore because he is gone Ashley. I know you loved him, but you deserve to move on to a new life. You are still young, beautiful and alive. James loved you with all his heart, but he wouldn't want you to live the rest of your life alone. James wouldn't worry about you doing something that would put Ashton in danger, because Ashton is your connection to James that you will see every time you look at him, but taking that ring off will be a big step in moving on," Venita said.

Ashley held her left hand out in front of her and then she removed the ring from her finger. Ashley kissed her wedding ring before taking it to the bedroom and placing it in her jewelry box.

"My hand feels so naked," Ashley said.

"I know. Let's go," Venita said as she took Ashley's hand.

Ashley and Venita went to a club south of downtown Dallas that catered to a predominantly adult African American clientele. This venue featured food and a live band. Ashley and Venita found a table away from the dance floor and ordered a few appetizers and a bottle of wine.

"I'm glad you came and dragged me out of the house. Most days I talk to a preschooler and a few folks by phone. Since all this stuff with the trial, agreement and interviews will die down soon I need to start living a normal life again," Ashley said.

"It looks like that normal life is coming your way. A tall, dark-skinned brother is coming straight for you right now," Venita said.

"What, you're kidding me," Ashley replied.

"Hello, ladies. I'm Benton Tate. May I sit with you for a moment?" Benton asked.

"Sure. Sit down. I'm Venita and this is Ashley," Venita said.

"It's nice to meet you," Ashley said.

"I'm the owner of this club and wanted to make sure you are having a good time," Benton said.

"You own the place. I don't want to sound skeptical, but you seem a little young to own a place like this?" Ashley said.

"Don't worry. I get that all the time. I got my college degree in hospitality and worked for one of the major hotel chains. I moved up the ladder, but decided I wanted to run my own show. I saved my money, kept my credit clean and when this place was failing under previous ownership I was able to scope it up, make some changes and turn it around. I'm thirty, but my long term goal is to open a Black owned hotel in downtown Dallas," Benton said.

"That's ambitious," Ashley said.

"I know, but it good to have goals. You know, you look so familiar for some reason," Benton said to Ashley.

"You probably saw her on television. Ashley is my sister-in-law. She was married to my brother, James Thomas, who was shot by that woman cop off Loop 12," Venita said.

"You know, that is where I saw you. I'm so sorry about what happened to your husband. I followed that so closely. That could happen to me. You were great and never stopped until you got something done. Some people don't understand that the first step is getting rid of the bad apples on police forces and keeping them off. Things are still going to happen, but that's a good place to start. I'm so glad I met you. We talked about what happened to your husband for a long time around here. I'm taking care of everything for you tonight. Listen I have an event I'd like to invite you to as a guest, here's my card. Call me tomorrow and I'll give you the details," Benton said as he stood to leave.

"Well, thank you," Ashley said.

Benton walked away and greeted other patrons at their tables.

"He was nice," Ashley said.

"Um Humm," Venita said with a raised eyebrow.

"What does that mean," Ashley said.

"He was nice because he liked what he saw," Venita said.

"I think he was just being a gentleman," Ashley said.

"Ashley, have you lost all your instincts about men. That man was throwing you across this table in his mind. He wants you. You got that sexy mature woman thing going on right now. A good looking mid-thirty year old woman gets younger guys like him curious. They want to know what you can teach them or what they can show you," Venita said.

"I think he was just being nice," Ashley said.

"Are you going to call him?" Venita said.

"I might, just to see what he's talking about. Would you call him?" Ashley asked.

"Hell yeah, I'd call him. Did you see that tight ass he had when he was walking away? A man with ass muscles like that will knock your back out. You hadn't had your spine adjusted in a long time," Venita said.

"Venita! You're so nasty," Ashley said with a laugh.

"You knew how nasty I was when you and James walked in on me and Dashon in that cabana on that beach in Florida. Man, he was rocking my ass that night, too bad he couldn't keep his dick in his pants and was even trying to fuck my daughter behind my back. She told me about him coming on to her and I kicked his ass to the curb," Venita said.

"Venita, I didn't know about that. What a piece of shit," Ashley said.

"That's all right. You had enough to deal with on your own. I'm not looking to fall in love anymore. I've got a thirty one year old cuddy buddy. When I need it, he comes over and puts it on my ass and goes home. I don't have to put up with any of that other bullshit. If a real man comes along and we connect, so be it. I'm tired of weeding through garbage trying to find gold. He can find me," Venita said.

"Amen to that sister," Ashley said as she held her wine glass up and made a toast with Venita.

"In the mean time you might want to see if Mr. tall, dark and handsome can knock the dust off that coochie of yours," Venita said.

"Venita, you're terrible, but I'll call him tomorrow," Ashley said with a smile.

21

It was twelve noon on a Saturday and Ashley picked up Benton's business card and looked at it for a long time. Ashton was sitting in the family room playing a video game. Ashley nervously dialed Benton's number and was almost fearful that he would answer.

"Hello," Benton's smooth baritone voice said.

"Hello, is this Benton?" Ashley asked.

"Yes, it is," Benton replied.

"This is Ashley Thomas. I met you at your club last night," Ashley reminded.

"Yes, Ashley, I remember. I'm so glad you called. I wanted to invite you to a little gathering I'm having at the Dallas Ponies' basketball game tonight. I've rented a suite and invited some of my friends and business associates. I thought you might want to hang out and relax," Benton said.

"You're a basketball fan? I like basketball. It sounds like fun," Ashley replied.

Benton gave Ashley the details and she called a teenage neighbor that acted as Ashton's babysitter when she needed to be away from home at night. Ashley felt relieved that Benton didn't asked for a one on one date or something along those lines because she didn't feel she was ready for that type of interaction with a man. Like a teenage girl, Ashley called Venita and told her about Benton inviting her to the professional basketball game. After getting off the phone with Venita, Ashley heard her doorbell ring. Ashley answered the door.

"Janeka, what are you doing here? Why didn't you call?" Ashley asked.

"I knew you would be home. You don't hardly go anywhere anymore," Janeka said.

"Am I that bad," Ashley said.

"Yes you are. Ashton come here and give auntie Janeka some sugar," Janeka said as Ashon ran over and planted a kiss on her cheek.

"For your information, I'm going out tonight," Ashley said.

"With a man?" Janeka questioned.

"Well yeah, kinda. I met a guy last night and he invited me to the Ponies' basketball game tonight. It's not a date, but he rented a suite and will have some of his friends there too," Ashley informed.

"He rented a suite. That's not cheap. Who is this man?" Janeka asked.

"His name is Benton Tate," Ashley said as she looked at his business card.

"Damn girl, you got to look at a card. Benton Tate, doesn't he own that nightclub just south of downtown?" Janeka asked.

"Yeah, do you know him," Ashley asked.

"I don't know him, but I know of him from a couple of my friends. It seems he's a real catch and he hasn't bitten on their bait. You've met my friend Sherika, you know, big ass and titties and always wearing the tightest shit she can get into. She said she went out with him once and she let him know he could get it and he didn't want it. Sherika thinks he has a little sugar in his tank because of that. I think he just didn't want to deal with a thot," Janeka said.

"What's a thot?" Ashley asked.

"Ashley, you're joking right? A thot means that hoe over there. Sherika was acting like that hoe over there by trying to fuck the man on a first date. So he may not like thots, maybe he like milfs," Janeka said.

"Okay, what's a milf?" Ashley asked.

"That's what you are. Milf means, mother I'd like to fuck," Janeka said.

"Oh my God. That's terrible," Ashley said with a laugh.

"You're laughing now, but he might want some of mama's goodies," Janeka said.

"Okay. I get it. All men have sex on the brain, but I just met him and this is hardly a one on one date. I'm just going to try and have some fun for a change," Ashley said.

"Okay. I'm just having some fun. I'm glad to see a smile on your face after everything you've gone through. I miss you so much at work," Janeka said.

"I know. I miss my career too, but I had to do what I did for James and Ashton. Ashton might be half White, but you how it is, the world will see him as a Black man. It's really scary to think about. I hope Ashton doesn't have the same thing happen to him that happened to James. I think about it all the time," Ashley said.

"I know and there's nothing I can say to ease your worry, because you lived it. Hey, I was just stopping by. You have a good time tonight. I've got to run. Love you girl," Janeka said as she and Ashley hugged each other.

Ashley looked at the time and realized it was time to get herself together so she could arrive at the game on time. Ashley decided to go with a pair of tight white pants, form fitting black top and strapless high heeled sandals. Ashley got Ashton situated with his babysitter before giving him a kiss on his cheek before she left. After navigating traffic, parking and picking up her pass, Ashley finally walked into the suite where Benton greeted her.

"Ashley you made it. Come on in. There's plenty of food and drinks. Make yourself at home," Benton said.

Ashley was impressed and surprisingly relaxed. Benton had an eclectic group of friends and business associates. Ashley was sitting near the viewing area watching the game when Benton sat down next to her.

"Are you having a good time?" Benton inquired.

"You know Benton, this is the second time in two nights that you've asked me if I'm having a good time. Yes, I'm having a great time. Thanks for inviting me, but I do have a question. Why did you invite me?" Ashley said.

"Once I found out who you were, I wanted to get to know you better, so I invited you here so I could spend more time with you. I admired your determination and focus after what happened to your husband. I like women of substance trying to make a difference in the world and it doesn't hurt if they are as beautiful as you are as an added bonus," Benton said.

"Mr. Tate, you have a way with words, but thank you. I haven't been getting out very much since everything happened with my husband so this is a welcome change. I'm sorry, I don't mean to reference everything around that event, but it's like it became this before and after dividing point in my life," Ashley said.

"Look you have no reason to apologize to me. It's understandable to feel that way. My mother passed away from cancer five years ago and I think of my life in a before and after her death the same way. I get it," Benton said.

"I'm sorry to hear that, but you do get it, don't you?" Ashley said.

"Yes, I do. I'm going to ask you something and I will understand if you say no. I would like to take you out for dinner sometime. Anywhere you want. Anytime you want. No pressure. Just call me when you're ready," Benton said.

"Thanks. I'll think about that," Ashley said.

Ashley enjoyed the rest of the night and drove home with thoughts of what would come next in her life outweighing those of what happened in the past for the first time she could remember since James was shot. Ashley went through the next week doing her usual routine, until she saw a review on a seafood restaurant positioned on the top floor of the tallest building in Dallas. Ashley took out her phone and called Benton.

"I'm ready to go to dinner," Ashley said.

Ashley told Benton where she wanted to go and he said he would set it up and call her back later. One hour later Benton called Ashley and told her he had made reservations for the next Saturday night at the restaurant she told him about. Ashley had ample time to make arrangements for Ashton and decide how she would approach the first real date she would have with a man since James died from his wounds about one and a half years before. Ashley realized how long it had been since she thought of herself a just a woman apart from being a mother and widow. Ashley walked over to a full length mirror mounted on her bathroom wall and looked at her image.

Given that she was now in her mid-thirties, Ashley was still a very attractive woman. Ashley kept her body in shape with vigorous exercise and a careful diet, but she did notice a few areas that showed her age. Small lines around the edge of her mouth and slight lines at the corners of Ashley's eyes were signs of maturity that she never really noticed until that moment. Overall Ashley thought she felt and looked good given what she had been through emotionally.

The days melted away and Ashley once again met Benton at the location they selected. Ashley didn't quite feel comfortable with having a man she didn't really know pick her up at her home so soon after they met. Ashley walked into the restaurant and Benton was waiting for her.

"Wow, you look great." Benton said.

"Thank you. You dress up nice yourself," Ashley said.

The food didn't disappoint and was fabulous.

"This place is nice," Ashley said.

"Yes it is and so are you. So, tell me about Ashley Thomas," Benton said.

Ashley told Benton about her background and even how she came to have a preference for Black men.

"That is very interesting and how has that been for you in general?" Benton asked.

"It's been fine, but I have received backlash for my choices. Of course the biggest one is what happened to my husband. I think he would still be alive if he wasn't Black," Ashley said.

"Ashley, I'm sorry. I didn't mean to be insensitive. I wasn't thinking," Benton said.

"No Benton, it's fine. That's a part of who I am now. I think about how cruel some of the people out there were after James was shot. They called me names and disrespected him because we were a mixed race couple. Let's talk about something else. Tell me about you," Ashley asked.

Benton told Ashley how he grew up and came to be where he was now.

"I would have never thought you grew up in the inner city. I don't mean to sound like I'm expecting some kind of hood stereotype, but I thought you were from the suburbs," Ashley said.

"Okay, so I give off a suburban vibe," Benton said with a laugh.

"That's not what I mean. You're very polished for a man your age," Ashley said.

"Oh wow, now I'm a wet behind the ears soft suburban brother. I'll take that as a complement. I always said we can be born in the ghetto, but the ghetto is not born in us," Benton said.

"Well, I can drink to that because I feel the same way about my younger years. We both escaped to better lives," Ashley said.

"As for the wet behind the ears thing, maybe I'll get a chance to dispel that perception," Benton said.

"If you're lucky," Ashley said.

Benton was taken aback by Ashley's response.

"Well, I don't have a comeback for that," Benton said as he took a drink.

About thirty minutes later Benton walked Ashley to her car in the parking garage.

"I had a great time Benton. Thank you," Ashley said.

"So did I, but I want to see you again. How about next Saturday around five at my place? I'll cook dinner for you," Benton asked.

"You can cook?" Ashley asked.

"Absolutely, I went to culinary school," Benton said.

"Where do you live?" Ashley said.

"Above the club. I have a loft space up there. You'll love it," Bentley said and he paused.

Ashley didn't say a word for thirty seconds.

"Okay, it sounds like fun. I'll be there at five," Ashley said.

Ashley was about to turn to get into her car when Benton put his arms around her waist and pulled her body close to his.

"Benton…" Ashley said but she was cut off by his kiss.

Ashley felt the strong embrace of Benton and the strength in his body. Benton's soft lips touched Ashley's and she parted her lips and returned his attention. Ashley pulled away and looked Benton in his eyes.

"Bye," Ashley said as she sat in her car's driver's seat and drove away.

Ashley looked into her rear view mirror and saw Benton still standing there as she drove around the first turn to exit the parking garage. Ashley felt excited and somewhat afraid as she drove home. The next day Venita called Ashley and asked her how things went when she went to Benton's basketball gathering.

"You went out with him again. That sounds promising," Venita said.

"He kissed me," Ashley said.

"He kissed you. What did you do?" Venita asked.

"I was a little surprised, but I kissed him back. I liked it, plus I'm going over to his house next Saturday. Benton said he's going to cook dinner for me," Ashley asked.

"Really, that's date number three. You're moving pretty fast with him. After three dates he might want to get in your panties. I'm just saying," Venita said.

"Well, I'm a big girl. I'm not going to do anything I don't want to do. Shit, I'm thirty five and pushing thirty six now. Benton is five years younger than I am. We may not have much in common and this thing may just be a curiosity. We could end up looking at each other with nothing to talk about," Ashley said.

"I guess you're right. My little cuddy buddy likes rap music and video games. All we do when we get together is fuck. That's good enough for me and he can take his ass home after that," Venita said.

"Venita, you keep me laughing. As bad as we bumped heads when we first met, you're the best sister-in-law I could ever have," Ashley said.

"Thanks. I feel the same way. Okay. Well, I've got to run. Let me know if you get some next Saturday," Venita said.

"Bye Venita, with your silly ass," Ashley replied.

22

Ashley decided she would break with her past and purchased a new outfit to wear when went to Benton's house for dinner. It was the fall of the year and Ashley decided to go with a comfortable blue sun dress without sleeves. The daily temperatures were peaking in the middle eighty degree range. Fall had always been Ashley's favorite time of year in Texas as the summer heat had subsided and given way to comfortable days with just a touch of coolness in the mornings. A pair of four inch high heeled casual sandals completed Ashley's shopping spree.

When Ashley arrived back home her mother called to check on her and talk with Ashton. After talking with her young grandson, Katherine spoke with Ashley.

"Am I seeing anybody? Well kind of, I met a guy a few weeks ago and we've gone out a couple of times, but we don't know each other that well," Ashley said.

"Who is he and is he you know, like James," Katherine asked.

"What? His name is Benton and yes mama, he's Black like James. You know I like Black men and that hasn't changed. I just haven't really thought about men much at all and have focused on moving past everything that happened. I wanted to make sure Ashton was okay. He cried and asked about his daddy for a long time. I don't want him to forget James and have all kinds of pictures and videos that I have saved on my computer, but I'm afraid if I show them to him he will started asking for him again. Mama, he's young now, but one day he will see his father get shot on video. All he will have to do is look James' name up on the internet and it pops up. I can't control when that happens," Ashley said with her voice trembling.

"Ashley, that is something you can control. Children are so much smarter today than when I was growing up. My parents didn't talk to me about anything. When I got my period I was scared to death and though I had cancer or something because my mother never told me that would happen to me. You can shape how Ashton feels about James by showing him pictures and videos of all of you together. Christmas videos and how James was with him will help him have an idea of who his daddy was. When he is old enough, sit him down and talk to him about how James died. Showing him that video will allow you to control how he sees it. The last thing you want is for some kid in elementary school showing it to Ashton on a cell phone. Some kids are very mean now. I've never seen anything like it. You need to think about that," Katherine said.

"Mama, that makes sense. I never thought about somebody else just showing Ashton the video of James being shot out of the blue," Ashley admitted.

"Well, I've got to run. I'm making gumbo for tonight. Your father has one of his work friends coming over to watch college football tonight," Katherine said.

"Oh, I wish you could send me some through the phone. Bye mama. Love you," Ashley said.

"Love you too sweetie," Katherine said.

Ashley ended the call and looked over at Ashton who was anticipating his friend coming over to spend the night. Ashley knew her mother was right about how she should keep James memory alive for Ashton, including shaping the story of how he died before someone else did.

"Ashton, come here baby," Ashley called.

Ashton ran over to Ashley.

"Yeah mama," Ashton said.

Ashley picked up her tablet computer and opened a file folder on the screen.

"I want to show you something. Do you know who that is? Ashley asked.

"Daddy!" Ashton replied.

"Who is that your daddy is holding," Ashley asked.

"A baby," Ashton asked.

"That is you," Ashley replied.

"I'm not a baby. I'm a big boy now," Ashton said.

"Yes, you are a big boy now. Your daddy would be so proud of you," Ashley said.

"Is daddy still in Heaven?" Ashton said.

"Yes, your daddy is still in Heaven," Ashley replied.

"Will daddy come home from heaven?" Ashton asked.

"No, your daddy lives in Heaven now, but he can see you and loves you," Ashley said when the doorbell rang.

"That's Chad mama!" Ashton said.

Ashley dried a tear from her right eye before going to the door to greet Chad and his mother.

The week sped by and before she knew it Ashley was dropping Ashton off at Chad's house on Saturday as his parents were returning the favor and allowing Ashton to spend the night at their house. Ashley was dressed in the clothes she bought the week before and started the drive to Benton's place. Ashley called to let Benton know she was on her way. When Ashley pulled into the parking lot she called Benton and he told her to pull into the alley that ran behind the club to a driveway that led to a gate. The gate swung open and Ashley drove inside and parked. A garage door opened and Benton was standing there. Ashley got out of her car and greeted Benton.

"What is this setup?" Ashley asked.

"Well, in order for me to have some privacy and separation from the club, I built this gated off driveway with privacy barriers on both sides so everyone at the club can't see me coming and going. I've got a set of stairs that will take up to the loft. Come on up," Benton said.

Ashley followed behind Benton and noticed his new black Lincoln Continental and white Corvette Stingray. Ashley gulped when she saw the sports car that was similar to the one James was driving when he was shot. Once they entered the loft, Ashley was impressed.

"Wow, this is nice," Ashley said.

The feel of the space was very masculine with black marble floors, stainless steel appliances and European style furniture.

"Thank you. I did my best to make this a real home. I put in a lot of sound barrier material in the floor and walls to isolate the space from the sounds from the club below. I planted some heat resistant plants on the roof deck just outside, but the Texas heat in the middle of summer makes it tough to keep anything alive except for desert plant varieties," Benton said.

Benton gave Ashley a tour of his place and she noticed several unique art pieces, a reading area stocked with books and a whirlpool spa just beyond the outside glass doors of his bedroom. Benton's bedroom was sparse and elegant with a king size bed and an eighty-inch high definition television mounted on the wall.

"Come have a seat at the bar while I cook our meal," Benton said.

"This is quite a place," Ashley said as she sat at a barstool.

"Thank you. Okay Miss. What can I fix you to drink? Anything you want," Benton asked.

"Anything?" Ashley asked.

"Anything," Benton replied.

"Okay. I want a frozen strawberry margarita with salt on the rim," Ashley said.

"No problem," Benton said.

Benton proceeded to prepare the drink the same way a bartender would in his club below. Benton had a blender, all of the ingredients and chilled glasses in his freezer. Benton placed the completed drink on the bar in front of Ashley with a straw in the glass. Ashley took a drink.

"Oh, this is so good. I'm impressed," Ashley said.

"Thank you. I can do every job in my club, just in case someone can't make it in. I'm cooking a Cajun meal with blackened catfish and rice with shrimp and oysters in a wine sauce as a topping. I also have some gumbo for an appetizer. Dessert will be my own version of cheesecake and of course, wine to wash it all down," Benton said.

"That sounds delicious. I have to tell you I was cautious about coming. My social life has almost been nonexistent since what happened to my husband. I had to adjust to being a single mom on top of everything else that was going on in my life, but I'm glad I came. So I do have a question," Ashley asked.

"What is it?" Benton asked.

"Well, since your home is right above your club, have you brought any women you met there up here for a nightcap, if you know what I mean?" Ashley asked.

"I could see why you might think that. You know like the spider luring the fly into it web. The answer is no. That would be a bad idea and bad for business. I don't need any personal drama in the middle of my business, so I keep those two things separate. I'm not a player, by any means," Benton said.

"Really, I mean so many men, especially successful Black men, use their success to their advantage since a lot of women are looking for someone like you. I've run into guys in the past that had a string of women they were seeing," Ashley said.

"I'm familiar with that guy. I know that guy, but I'm not that guy. I don't have time for that if I plan to own that hotel one day. I'm very careful and selective in my relationships," Benton said as he took a sip of wine.

"Okay," Ashley said as he took a drink.

Ashley watched Benton as he went about preparing their meal.

"We are getting close to meal time. I'm turning on my vent since I'm about to blacken this fish. I've got my cast iron skillet very hot, my fish is coated in seasoning and the butter is dancing in the skillet. Here goes," Benton said as her dropped the fish filets into the skillet.

Smoke rose into the air as the fish sizzled in the skillet. The smell of the spices invaded Ashley's nostrils. Ashley and Benton moved to the dining room table and Benton brought out their meal.

"Well, it looks like we will have to eat our gumbo along with the rest of the meal," Benton said.

Benton blessed the food and Ashley took a bite of the fish.

"Umm, this is so good," Ashley said.

"Thank you. I try my best," Benton said.

Ashley and Benton had good food, good conversation and enjoyed each other's company.

At the end of the meal they moved to the living room and took a seat.

"I meant to tell you earlier that you look beautiful as always," Benton said.

"Thank you. When I came to the club with my sister-in-law, why did you come over and invite me to the basketball game?" Ashley asked.

"When I saw you, you seemed to be questioning why you were here. You were at ease, but didn't seem to be particularly interested in being there or anywhere else for that matter, so I really wanted to see if you were having a good time. I invited you to the game after I got close to you, saw your smile and found out who you were. I thought you needed to have a good time and I admired what you did. I find strong women attractive," Benton said.

"Thank you. I didn't choose to be strong, but I had to be. I kept thinking about what happened and even though I was married to a Black man, I would never know how it felt to have people fear or hate me just because of who they thought I was. I witnessed White women clutch their purses tighter or lock their car doors when James walked by, even when I was with him. Has that happened to you?" Ashley asked.

"Of course. I get followed in some stores and ignored when I walk into some high end retail shops. When I bought my sports car, I walked into a dealership and was looking at one on the showroom floor and no one came out to help me or anything. This White guy came in after I did and a sales guy walked by me and helped him. I found the sales manager and told him he had lost a sale. I already knew what I wanted when I walked in. I went somewhere else, was treated with respect and bought the car. After I got it, I drove up to first dealership called the sales manager out and showed him the sale he lost. It's a very demeaning and frustrating experience, but I know who I am and other people don't define me or determine my self-worth," Benton said.

"I had a similar experience when I was younger with others calling me White trash, but that doesn't happen anymore. I'm doing well and look like any other White person out there, but you can't do that in this society and neither could my husband. As much success as he achieved, he was always a Black man and someone with the power to take his life did so because of some unreasonable fear she had deep inside, that is what I will always believe," Ashley said as she stood and walked to a window facing south.

Ashley looked toward the north and could see the lights of downtown Dallas. Benton walked up and stood on side of her.

"What are you thinking about?" Benton asked.

"I'm watching the cars pulling into the parking lot and all the cars going up and down the freeway. Everybody is going somewhere they want to be. I haven't wanted to be somewhere in a long time. No one has needed me to be somewhere in a long time," Ashley said.

"That's not true. I wanted and needed you to be here," Benton said.

Benton stepped behind Ashley and placed his arms around her waist while kissing her neck from the back. Ashley felt his warm lips on her neck and his right hand on her left breast. Ashley turned and faced Benton. Benton leaned down and kissed Ashley deeply.

Feelings and sensations Ashley hadn't felt in many months began to stir inside her body and mind. Benton reached behind Ashley and pulled the zipper down on her dress and it fell down to her waist before falling to the floor. Benton pulled Ashley's bra downward and exposed her succulent breasts. Ashley gasped as Benton used his tongue and mouth to taste and tease her supple mounds.

"Oh Benton," Ashley said.

Benton didn't reply, but he moved downward and positioned himself on his knees in front of Ashley. Benton moved the crotch of her panties to the side and felt her soaking wet core. Benton's tongue tasted Ashley's nectar and she felt electric sensations shoot through her body.

"Oh God! Lick my pussy baby!" Ashley said as she lay against the window for support.

Benton had removed his clothing piece by piece as he attended to Ashley's needs. Ashley was thrusting her hips and grinding her pelvis into Benton's face. Benton then removed Ashley's panties and he stood while lifting Ashley into the air with her legs hooked into his arms. Ashley wrapped her arms around Benton's neck and then she felt him press her back up against the cool window glass while he began to go where no man had been in almost a year and a half. Benton slowly pressed his pelvis forward and Ashley's eyes widened as she welcomed his intrusion. Ashley locked her ankles around Benton's back. Benton pressed forward until he could no more and he paused.

"Oh shit. You're so deep in me baby!" Ashley said.

Benton then moved his hips back and slammed forward again and again.

"Shit, you're so tight!" Benton said.

Benton then walked back to his bedroom with Ashley draped around his body clinging on tightly. Benton lay on the bed with Ashley's body under his. Benton folded Ashley's legs back on his shoulders while his strong body was supported by his hands and toes on the bed as he drove into her core repeatedly. Benton's body slapped against Ashley's and the sound echoed throughout the loft space.

"That's it! That's it! Fuck me baby!" Ashley urged.

"Ungh! Ungh!" Benton exclaimed as he exploded inside Ashley and collapsed on top of her.

Ashley rolled Benton over. Ashley went into the bathroom and brought back a wet towel and cleaned up Benton and herself. Ashley then began to breathe life back into Benton's member because she wasn't quite finished yet.

"Suck that dick baby! Shit!" Benton said.

Ashley then stopped and mounted Benton with her back facing him. Ashley then began to slam her hips down on Benton's pelvis until she felt a welling up inside her about to burst through an emotional dam. Ashley noticed her image in a mirror mounted on a wall alongside the bed. Ashley looked at her image as she was grinding on top of that man. Ashley, for the first time in her life saw the full contrast of her white skin against that of a Black man as she picked up her pace. Suddenly Ashley went over the edge and watched her own climax in the mirror. With her back bowed and legs trembling, Ashley slammed down onto Benton's stiff member as if she was attempting to remove it from his body.

"Oh fuck! Give me that Black dick baby! Fuck this White pussy! Oh shit!" Ashley exclaimed as Benton grabbed her hips and grunted from somewhere deep inside.

Ashley didn't know if her relationship with Benton would go anywhere beyond that night, but she looked at herself in the mirror, thought of James and smiled.

About The Author

ESSENCE® bestselling author D.T. Pollard lives in the Dallas/Fort Worth, TX area. He is married and has one son.

Other works
By
D T Pollard
Rooftop Diva – A Novel of Triumph
After Katrina (fiction)
Fools' Heaven – Love, Lust and
Death Beyond the Pulpit (fiction)
TARP TOWN U S A – The
Recession That Saved America
OBAMA GUILTY OF BEING
PRESIDENT WHILE BLACK
Vampire Sapien
The Mark Unmasked
Publish Free For Kindle Today
Sell Worldwide Tomorrow
World Wide Nuclear Power Plant Guide
Unemployed But Not Destroyed
Vulture Capitalism
Whitney Houston – Poems for Whitney
Whitney Amy Michael Elvis
The Good Old Girls Club
President Obama – Diary of Disrespect
Who

Who Moved My Ocean – Avoid The Shrinking Job Trap

Mitt Romney's America – No Trespassing By The 47%

Romnesia – How Dangerous Is It

Obama 2.0

Carnage Control

Gold Digger's Grave

Things You Can't Tell Mama – The Pastor's Wife

Things You Can't Tell Mama – Her Man Was Once Yours

Things You Can't Tell Mama – Her Blond Best Friend

Things You Can't Tell Mama - Mr. Taboo

Things You Can't Tell Mama – The Prophetess Affair

Things You Can't Tell Mama–Your Best Friend's Mother

Things You Can't Tell Mama – The President's Sex Tape

Things You Can't Tell Mama – Anthology

Confessions of a Single Black Woman

Tiberius – Rap's Rainmaker

Things you Can't Tell Mama – The Pastor's Wife 2

Mommy Porn

Jacob's Cabin

The Pastor's Lover

Side Piece
Side Piece 2 – Amber Alarm
Hero In The Hood
The Pastor's Lover 2
She Twerks Hard For The Money
The Pastor's Lover 3
Forget Big Brother We Tell DAD
Everything
The Pastor's Wife 3
Hoe Hoe Hoe Merry Christmas
Ghetto Tony and White Trash Tina
Fifty Shades of Plaid
Grandma Does It Better
Keisha's Mama Is So Fine
Less Pretty
Pretty For A Dark Skinned Woman
Massive Monroe
The Pastor's Lover 4 – The Pastor's Wife 4
The Obituary of Gut Bucket Johnson
Forget Big Brother – We Tell DAD
Everything
Unreal Housewives of South Dallas
Liquid Memories: You Can Live Forever
Gold Digger's Game
Ebola – Partying With Grace
THOT On The Beach
What Would Dr King Think About Today's
Black America

Your Best Friend's Mother 2 – Lust In
London
Trump – Plutocracy & Apartheid USA
Secrets of a Baby Mama
Secrets of a Baby Mama 2
Trump – Nixon on Steroids – Stay Woke

www.ingramcontent.com/pod-product-compliance
Lightning Source LLC
Chambersburg PA
CBHW070915180626
46817CB00003B/1075